SWARM RISING

TIM PEAKE

and Steve Cole

HODDER CHILDREN'S BOOKS

First published in Great Britain in 2021 by Hodder and Stoughton
This paperback edition published in Great Britain in 2022

1 3 5 7 9 10 8 6 4 2

A CIP catalogue record for this book is available from the British Library.

PB ISBN 978 1 444 96086 0

Typeset in Kallisto by Avon DataSet Ltd, Arden Court, Alcester, Warwickshire

Printed and bound in Great Britain by Clays Ltd, Elcograf S.p.A.

The paper and board used in this book are made from wood from responsible sources.

Hodder Children's Books
An imprint of
Hachette Children's Group
Part of Hodder and Stoughton
Carmelite House
50 Victoria Embankment
London EC4Y 0DZ

An Hachette UK Company
www.hachette.co.uk

www.hachettechildrens.co.uk

TP – *For Thomas and Oliver,*
look what you started . . . the Swarm is here!

SC – *For Amy, always*

THEY'RE COMING . . .

It's time to get serious about aliens.

For years we've imagined aliens as little green people with enormous heads, big eyes, small bodies and long fingers. Perhaps we think this is how humans will evolve as we become more intelligent.

The truth is far more frightening than you could imagine.

In 1974 the human race hurled a message into outer space.

It was a signal sent out in radio waves towards a far corner of our galaxy. A signal aimed at alien beings, telling them that they were not alone in the universe. Telling them where the Earth could be found and what creatures ruled it.

The message was sent to celebrate human cleverness. No one really expected aliens to receive the message. To come looking for the Earth. To find us.

When the aliens arrive, they won't be in spacecraft. They'll travel at the speed of light, a signal in code, a hive of intelligence. The question is, who will hear them – and what do they want?

A swarm is rising.

Soon – very soon – it will be here.

FIVE YEARS
FROM NOW . . .

CHAPTER ONE
FIRST CONTACT

I'm Danny Munday, but my story starts on a Tuesday.

Hilarious, right? You can imagine the crummy jokes I've had to put up with at school my whole life, like: 'Oh, no, I thought it was Friday but here's Munday!' Or, 'Who puts the "weak" into weekday – Danny Munday!' Or, 'You're gonna marry Freya Knight so you can call yourself Danny Munday-Knight' – which doesn't even make sense because a) I wouldn't have to take her surname if I didn't want to and b) Freya Knight can break your bones just by looking at you so I would not mess.

Anyway. Back to Munday on that Tuesday.

It was just an ordinary night, you know? Mum out at work, homework half finished, Jamila round, being a pain . . . Nah, that's harsh. She's my best mate – I've known her all my life. We were in my room, playing

Breakout Saturn on PlayStation, stuffing Doritos and having a laugh.

Or we were until Jamila totally got me killed by giant alien spiders.

'Thanks a lot, Jam!' I whacked her on the arm. 'You're meant to be Captain Maxima Layne, fearless Queen of the Spaceways – why did you run? The noise brought every Spidroid for miles coming!'

'You were a sacrifice I was willing to make, Danny-boy!' Jamila laughed. 'I don't have to outrun the Spidroids – I only have to run faster than you!'

'Get a life, Jam.' I tossed the controller down in mock disgust. 'It's my turn to play as Maxima next and I'm totally gonna get *you* killed.'

'We both know that won't happen.' She grinned. 'Chill! I'll make it up to you some day, Munday.'

'Sure you will. Anyway, it's nearly nine o'clock,' I told her. 'And you know what that means.'

'Oh, yeah. Totally.' Jamila hit pause on the game, bug-eyed spider-monsters all around her. 'Time to stop playing so I can go home to bed for a nice early night, ready for school tomorrow . . .'

We both broke out laughing. This *never* happens! Jamila only lives next door – it's a terraced street and our bedrooms are actually either side of the same wall. Sometimes we send morse code messages to each other by knocking on the plaster. Most times there's no need though, cos – a couple of times a week – Jamila goes back home like a good girl on the dot of nine, gets ready for bed and says goodnight to everyone.

Then, the minute her mum shuts the door, she slings on her jeans, climbs out through her window, uses the drainpipe to swing herself on to my windowsill and comes in through my window to finish the game, along with most of the Doritos. Then she sneaks back home again the window-way, nearer to midnight. We call it her SWIMMER trick – SWIMMER being short for 'Secret Window Into Mundays' Mansion, Emergency Route', obvs.

It's cool. We've gotten away with it for months: Jamila's mum and dad think their daughter's a perfect well-behaved angel so they never bother to check her room, and my mum is never around to notice. She works the late shift most nights. She's a researcher in radioastronomy, based at the Lovell Telescope at Jodrell Bank. It's pretty impressive, though it doesn't look much like a telescope to me – more like a giant's TV satellite dish.

That's cos you don't look through a radio telescope with your eyes. It's used to study energy in the universe that we can't see – radio waves, X-rays, microwaves, ultraviolet light and other stuff. When I was little, Mum explained her job by saying, 'It's a noisy universe out there – I work out what's worth listening to, and why.'

Dad's a professor in physics and astronomy, so he and Mum speak the same language. Unfortunately, they also *shout* the same language when they're together, which led to them splitting up and Dad taking a job at the Institute for Astronomy in Honolulu, cos he needed 'to get away'. Which, you know, sucked when it happened, but over the last two years we've all got used to it. I chat to him a lot online, usually when Mum is on the night shift; after Dad left, Mum threw herself into her work and it's been holding her pretty tight ever since.

Which is why I got such a shock when Mum came home early that night.

It was ten-past nine when me and Jamila levelled up, and I was just walking her downstairs to say 'Bye for now' when I heard the key turn in the front door. I actually jumped in the air, throwing Doritos all over the hall just as Mum bustled in. She had her laptop under her arm, a key in one hand and coffee in the other. She looked at us with bright, super-caffeinated eyes.

'Hey, Danny. Hi, Jam.' She scooped up a couple of chips from the carpet and munched them down. 'Sorry to interrupt. Were you about to snog each other goodbye?'

'What!' I flushed red – Mum is *so* embarrassing. 'No!'

'Gross,' said Jamila, holding her stomach.

'Like you'd ever admit it to me anyway.' Mum laughed and swigged the last of her coffee. 'Just pretend I'm not here.'

I mouthed 'Sorry!' to Jamila. Mum was in one of her manic moods; that meant she was either super-excited or super-exhausted. Probably both.

'Why *are* you here, Mum?' I asked. 'Your shift shouldn't finish for ages.'

'Couldn't get any work done there,' Mum said, barging through to the kitchen and whacking her laptop on the counter. 'The computers have been taken offline.'

'At Jodrell Bank, you mean?' I shrugged at Jamila, and we both followed her through. 'How come?'

'Some kind of power surge.' Mum crossed to the fridge and pulled out an open bottle of wine. 'We were picking up some very weird fast radio bursts when, BOOM! Something went through the systems. Took down the main server.' She studied the dirty glasses by the sink, shrugged, and poured the wine into her coffee cup. 'It wasn't just us affected. Radio telescopes in South Africa, Canada, Western Australia – they're all offline.'

'Freaky,' I said, kind of interested in Mum's work for once. 'Were the other telescopes listening to these fast radio bursts too?'

'What even *is* a fast radio burst?' Jamila said. 'Like, when you switch a radio on and off really quickly?'

Mum gave her a look, then took a gulp of wine. 'FRBs

are tiny blazes of energy, usually from distant galaxies. We're not sure what causes them, but they hardly ever repeat.' She frowned. 'But! This FRB did. Regular as clockwork. Energy waves rat-a-tatting through space at the speed of light. And the source was *really* close – just twenty-five light years away.'

Rat-a-tatting. For some reason I thought of me and Jamila tapping code to each other on our walls. 'Maybe it's a kind of message?'

'Ha – you mean a message to our IT department to protect the network with a stronger firewall?' She gave a laugh but I could tell it was totally fake. 'At least I captured part of the signal before the power surge. I'm going to analyse the pattern on my laptop. I'm sure there's a normal explanation.'

'Speaking of normal explanations, I'd better find one for my mum.' Jamila was looking at her phone. 'She's texting. I'm fifteen minutes late.'

'Tell her you were snogging Danny,' Mum suggested.

'Mum, *shut up*!' I groaned, steering Jamila out of the kitchen and back towards the front door. 'I'm sorry about her.'

'So cringe,' said Jamila. Then she smiled. 'At least your mum is fun.'

'Weird, you mean,' I corrected her. 'D'you still want to come round later? We've got Titan level to complete.'

'Better not. If your mum realises I'm here, she really will think we're snogging.' Jamila shuddered as she opened the front door. 'I'll see you tomorrow, yeah?'

'Yeah,' I said, stood on the doorstep. 'Prob text you later.'

'Prob read it.' She gave me a shove backwards and swung herself over the little fence dividing our front paths.

I closed the door and walked back to the kitchen. Mum had stuck a USB drive into her laptop. It flashed as if mimicking the fast radio burst as it transferred the data across. A progress bar on the screen began to fill.

'Weird how the computers at the other radio telescopes were taken down too,' I remarked. 'Maybe it was some sort of cyberattack?'

'Maybe.' Mum drummed her fingers on the countertop, waiting for the data to load. 'That's certainly more likely than one alternative explanation.'

'Which is?'

'That extragalactic energy could hit the Earth with enough force to affect our systems. A big, hard hello from outer space.'

'You mean it *could* be a message from aliens?' I breathed.

Mum looked up at me and snorted. 'That would be exciting, wouldn't it? But no, I'm sure there's a natural explanation. You know, back in the 1960s, strong, regular signals a bit like this were detected. It was thought that they might be messages from extraterrestrials.'

'And were they?'

'No, the radio waves were being thrown out by a stellar remnant.'

'The last remains of a star, you mean?' Yeah, you can call me a geek, but growing up with two astronomers means it's hard to miss this stuff. 'There are different types, aren't there?'

'This one was named a pulsar – just tens of miles across but still heavier than the Sun.' She shook her head. 'There's so much we still don't know about what's out there in space. The team that discovered pulsars got a Nobel Prize and all sorts of other goodies . . .'

I bit at her words like a hungry dog. 'Cash? Fast cars? Fame?'

'Decent grants for further research, at least.' The progress bar filled up with a soft chime and Mum turned back to the laptop screen, opening a file. 'Whatever this is . . . it could be *very* big.'

'Change-the-world big?' I asked her.

Mum didn't answer, lost in her work already. Although the data had loaded, the light on the USB drive was flashing madly, faster than ever, like a tiny fluttering heartbeat.

Then the little light went out, and I went out too, heading upstairs to my room.

Messages from outer space? Yeah, right. About as likely as me going out with Freya Knight.

Still, someone was certainly about to come into my life.

Or some*thing*.

CHAPTER TWO
ALARM BELLS

I went back to *Breakout Saturn* for a bit, but I'd promised Jamila I wouldn't take Captain Maxima through Titan Level without her so I couldn't do much except finish a few side missions. Maxima is like this future eco-warrior trying to turn Titan – Saturn's biggest moon – into a new Earth once our own gets too toxic. But evil alien spiders locked up in a floating prison in Saturn's gas clouds break out and make their base on Titan first. (I know – *typical*, right?) And the side missions usually involve Maxima terraforming Saturn's other moons – transforming barren rocks into miniature Earths that can support life – so that's kind of fun too.

It's always worried me that when our *real* Earth gets too polluted, moving to Titan isn't really an option, killer alien spiders or not.

Anyway, after making Titan greener, I strayed a little closer to home. There's this new park with the most amazing zip wire I want to go on – longest in the world, almost two miles through epic forest. Mum promised that maybe for my birthday we could go; I sent her a link to a couple of videos. You've got to keep the pressure on, right?

A message pinged back from Mum almost straight away. But it was blank.

I shrugged, and typed back: *You are speechless cos zip wire looks so awesome right?*

But just then my phone grew hot. So hot it actually hurt my hand. Then my apps started quitting and reloading. 'Weird,' I muttered. Maybe the battery was overheating? I dumped the phone on my bedside table.

Bored, I knocked on the wall – four times. It's short code for 'Hi, are you receiving?'

There was silence. Then a few seconds later my tablet pinged a notification. Jamila had messaged me: *Can't be bothered to morse knock :D*

I tutted. She cheats all the time now. When we were

younger she took things more seriously. She even learned morse faster than I did. Although to be fair, I guess we didn't have phones then.

You're lazy and useless, I messaged back. Then I added a *;)* cos I felt bad.

Her reply: *See? You can't morse-knock a passive-aggressive winky face.*

Then she added a *;)* too.

I knocked 'Get a life' on the wall.

Then my tablet pinged. Mum had replied. She was never normally this on top of things.

I opened the mail, but it was empty again. Nothing there.

'She's losing it,' I muttered. 'Big time.'

Then the tablet's screen turned black. I saw a cursor flash. Then green numbers typed themselves along the screen, as if a program was running:

01100111 01100101 01110100 00100000
01100001 00100000
01101100 01101001 01100110 01100101

'What the . . . ?' I stared at the ones and zeroes, then took a screen shot.

Just in time, as a moment later they were gone. I knew I would need to send pics as evidence if my tablet was breaking down as well as my phone . . .

Even as I thought of it, my phone suddenly buzzed. It was restarting all by itself. 'What is going on?' I said out loud.

Cautiously I picked up my phone. It wasn't hot any more. At the same time I noticed that my tablet had lost the black screen and was back to normal.

'Glitch Central,' I muttered, as a WhatsApp notification came through. It warned me the sender was not in my contacts list.

True enough, I didn't recognise the phone number. But the sender's name was apparently ADI.

'Who on earth is Adi?' I muttered.

The message was:

.... . .-.. .-.. ---   -.. .- -. -. -.—

I knew in a moment that it was morse code. The dots and dashes spelled, 'Hello Danny.'

Suspicious, I looked at the wall behind me, as if I'd be able to see Jamila laughing on the other side. This had to be her playing a joke. I morse-knocked on the wall: 'Funny. How u do that?'

The knocks came back. 'Do wot?'

'Text as Adi,' I knocked back.

'Adi wot?' came the reply.

OK. Option a), Jamila was playing dumb so she could wind me up some more, or option b), she really hadn't done it. In case it was option a), I decided not to say any more to Jamila so she wouldn't have the satisfaction of knowing I was weirded out.

Instead I WhatsApped 'Adi'.

Who is this? I asked.

Just a girl called Adi, came the swift reply, only in English this time. *I love code. You love code too?*

Every alarm bell in my head started ringing. A stranger had got hold of my number somehow and was trying to talk to me. Maybe the glitches in my phone and tablet meant I'd been hacked? Maybe it was linked to the computers at Jodrell Bank going down?

I got up, deciding to show Mum. But Adi stopped me in my tracks with another text:

Kash gave me your number. I'm his cousin Adi. He said you love code. I love code. Hello Danny

'Gee, thanks, Kash,' I said out loud. 'Ask me before handing out my number, why don't you!'

Kash is a mate of mine, though I haven't seen him for months since he started at the private school across town. Kash does know I'm into codes; we made up a cipher last year and used it to send each other secret texts about people at school. But we stopped when Mr Johnson, our Computer Studies teacher, caught us texting, cracked the cipher and realised we were making fun of his big nose.

That teacher who busted you 2 sounds a total douche, Adi added.

I smiled. I remembered Kash saying exactly that; he must have told his cousin.

I fired him off a quick text message: *Hey, butthead!*

You giving out my number? Your cousin Adi just got in touch. Kind of weird?

Kash replied straight away. *Hey, butthead. Adi cool. Thought you two make good friends.* There was a pause, then another message: *Be nice. You will like.*

It sounded like an order. I'm not great at taking orders.

I flipped back to Adi on WhatsApp. I typed: *Why text me? Don't u have real friends?* Then I felt bad so I added a LOL.

It's hard being a 14-year-old girl genius, lol, said Adi. *I should get a life!*

That made me smile. 'Get a life' is one of my favourite things to say. Maybe I really would like her.

A message came through from Jamila: *Night. See ya 2moro.*

At the same time, Adi WhatsApped me again: *Help me get a life, Danny?*

I stared at the screen. This was new. Kind of weird. Kind of cool.

Me and Adi spent the next hour chatting over text.

It was only at midnight that I remembered I hadn't said goodnight back to Jam.

And I didn't remember the glitching binary code on my tablet at all.

Maybe if I had, and if I'd showed that screenshot to Mum sooner, things wouldn't have gotten so badly out of control.

CHAPTER THREE
HACKED

As I found out over the next couple of days, it was mad how much Adi and I had in common. Her parents were scientists. She was veggie. She'd been to the same school camp as me in Year Six. She loved zip-wire rides, like I did. She loved gaming; we both played as Maxima Layne on *Breakout Saturn* and we had the same attitude to earning trophies – you've got to go for platinum, or else why bother?

She'd even been dragged along to climate-change marches like me. I told her how Mum only took me cos she was meeting friends in London and couldn't leave me at home, but Adi said saving the planet was something she could get behind. And I agreed. Because, well, no Titan – am I right?

Talking to Adi gave me something to do in the evenings. Mum stayed working from home, analysing all her terabytes of data, and it was down to me to get takeaways for our dinner – not that Mum remembered to eat much of hers. When she's totally into her work it's like she forgets the real world exists. Me included.

It's fine. I get that she loves her job and that she's happiest with a head full of radio waves. And sooner or later she'll remember she's got a son and will feel dead guilty and that, my friends, is when the world's longest zip wire will become a reality, so it's all cool.

Jamila thinks it's less cool. With Mum around she's not up for doing SWIMMER, just in case she's seen here and my mum tells her mum and Jam's grounded forever. So she's doomed to nine o'clock bedtimes for the foreseeable. Which is pretty much as bad as being grounded anyway.

So, given Jam has after-school clubs Wednesday and Thursday, it was Friday before I told Jamila about Adi in any detail as we walked back from school. I was kind of dreading it; it's not the easiest thing to say you've sparked up a conversation with a teenage girl you've never met before.

Sure enough, Jamila wasn't impressed.

'The whole thing sounds totally sus,' she said. 'I mean, some girl appears out of nowhere—'

'She's Kash's cousin!' I protested.

'Whoever's cousin she is, she wants a no one like you to help her get a social life?'

'Adi says she comes from a really big family. She's had to move from place to place her whole life.' I could hear how defensive I sounded, and it bugged me. 'I dunno, I guess it's lonely, having to live in different places, never getting to know people.'

Jam snorted. 'Why would she want to chat *you* up?'

'Jealous?' I grinned at her. 'You are, aren't you? Totally.'

'Yeah, and there's a pig flying out of my butt too.' Jamila mimed sticking her fingers down her throat. 'How much do you really know about this Adi, anyway?'

'I know loads,' I argued. But thinking about it, I only really knew what we had in common, not a thing about our differences. I'd gone hunting for her on social media but there was no trace, so I'd messaged Kash about that.

He'd messaged back saying that Adi didn't want people to see how few followers she had. I could relate to that.

Something else we had in common.

'Have you ever seen her picture?' Jamila persisted.

'Yeah.' I showed her the image I'd downloaded to my photos. 'See, she looks a bit like Maxima Layne from *Breakout Saturn*. Kind of.'

'I guess.' Jamila studied the slightly blurry image of a girl about our age with long black hair in a ponytail, chin pushed out and fingers held up in a sideways peace sign. 'Danny, this could be photoshopped. Adi could be some creepy bloke called Adrian for all you know!'

'What?' I groaned. 'I'm not stupid.'

'Ha!' said Jamila. 'Has *Adrian* asked to meet you somewhere yet?'

'No, *Adi* hasn't.' I swiped my finger across the screen. 'Look, here's another pic of her.'

This one showed Adi in the park, standing heroically with hands on hips and one leg hooked behind her. 'Oh god, she's doing the Maxima Layne victory stance.' Jamila snatched my phone to hold it out of the light and shook her head. 'Grim! Let me guess, she knows you play as Maxima.'

'She plays as Maxima too!' I protested.

'Course she does.' Jamila stopped walking and looked at me. 'Does she know that's my avatar too? Does she know about us?'

'Us?' I frowned, tried to get my phone back, but she held it out of reach. 'What us?'

'You and me, best mates – you idiot.' She pushed my shoulder. 'Have you told her about us?'

'I might have mentioned this annoying girl who keeps giving me a hard time,' I said. Truth was, I *had* told Adi a lot about Jamila. I'd even suggested we all hang together sometime, but Adi hadn't jumped at the chance. So much for wanting a life.

Or maybe it was only me she was interested in?

Suddenly my phone buzzed. I lunged for my phone but Jamila turned her back on me. 'Oooh, she's messaged you for, like, the five thousandth time . . .'

I grabbed her arm. 'Give it back, Jam!'

'Well, well.' Jamila turned to me, eyebrows raised.

'Looks like your new mystery friend wants to take things to the next level after all.'

'What?' I took the phone and stared at Adi's message:

I need you to meet me. Soon. Stand by.

'OK.' I swallowed. 'A meet. OK, that's cool.'

'Bit pushy – "*soon*",' Jamila said. 'You gonna meet her then?'

I shrugged. 'Guess so.'

'You can't go by yourself. What if it *is* dodgy?' She sounded serious. 'I'll go with you. Check Adi out.'

'To see if you approve?'

'To see if she's real!' Jamila retorted. 'Once I know you're all right, I'll leave you alone, if you want.'

'You can come and you can stay. Please?' I smiled at Jamila. 'You're a good mate.'

'Ugh, pass the sick bucket!' Jamila gave me a shove to propel me along the street. 'Now come on. Home. I need to be out of this uniform and into a onesie by five o'clock, latest . . .'

Me and Jamila said bye at our front doors. 'I'll let you know when the meet is,' I told her.

'And I'll let you know if I'm washing my hair,' she told me. With a wave, she vanished through the front door.

I guess I was feeling kind of excited. I mean, I got on with Adi over WhatsApp but we'd never actually talked to each other. It could turn out to be horrible, both of us tongue-tied while Jamila talked rubbish to fill the silence . . . Or maybe it would be cool, and all three of us would just click straight away and happily chill together.

One thing that clearly was *not* chill was my mum. I found her in the kitchen with the blinds down surrounded by about a hundred coffee cups and fifty plates with toast crusts, her hair wild and eyes kind of glazed over.

I knew the signs. This was a severely sleep-deprived mum who, when she finally crashed and woke again, would be ready to grant her poor neglected son a stack of treats, even though he did not really feel neglected at all (except he *was* poor, because Mum always forgot my allowance in times of stress and I'd already blown the monthly cash Dad gave me on games).

'Danny!' she cried. 'About time you showed up. You'll be late for school.'

'School's finished, Mum,' I said gently. 'And tomorrow's the weekend. Two days off, yeah?'

'Well, all right,' said Mum vaguely. 'But you'd best get there all the earlier on Monday morning.'

I suddenly noticed my tablet was on the kitchen counter, hooked up to Mum's big PC *and* her laptop. There were so many cables twisted around it might've been hooked up to the coffee machine as well.

'What are you up to, Mum?' I asked her in that same wary tone she'd used on me a thousand times before.

'I've chained our computers together. Extra processing power,' Mum explained with a manic grin. 'The fast radio burst that knocked out the computers – you know? Well, the diagnostics show many repeated elements, and *that* suggests it's some kind of code repeated over and over. This really could be a message from an extraterrestrial civilisation!' She laughed and held me close in a big hug that smelled of espresso and toast crumbs. 'Aliens, Danny! Imagine that!'

'It can't be,' I said. 'An actual signal? From actual aliens?'

'If it really is a code, and I can crack it . . .' Mum stared into the distance and yawned. 'Oh! Speaking of code, I didn't know you were learning binary notation. Very good.'

I frowned. 'What about binary?'

'That screenshot on your tablet,' she said. 'The code.'

I remembered the numbers appearing on my screen out of nowhere. 'What code?'

'Well, it's got to be you who wrote it, hasn't it?' She beamed and called it up on my tablet. '01100111 01100101 blah-ble-blah . . . In binary code it spells, "Get a life".'

Suddenly it felt hard to breathe. I remembered: I'd just morse-knocked 'Get a life' to Jamila through the wall when the numbers had zapped on to the screen.

And a minute later, 'Hello Danny' had appeared from Adi in dots and dashes – another kind of binary code. And then in English . . .

Mum had just told me that extraterrestrials could be

beaming messages through space, but all I could think was, *It can only have been Adi that left that code.* She hacked into my tablet.

And if she had access to that she could see all my pictures, all my email, all my personal information.

I felt cold. I'd been thinking me and Adi had so much in common. But it's not hard to fake all that when you've got access to someone's digital life history.

I decided it was time to talk to Kash and find out what was really going on. I scrolled through my contacts, found his number and hit call.

Nothing happened. It wouldn't connect.

Trying to keep calm, I picked up the landline and phoned from there. The dialling tone was reassuringly loud in my ear, purring like a digital cat.

Then the phone went dead before my call could connect.

Without a word, I threw open the front door, ran to Jamila's house and rang the doorbell. Her older brother answered with a grunt and I pushed past him. 'Jam!' I shouted. 'Jam, I need your phone.'

She was coming down the stairs in a polar bear onesie, looking at me like I was crazy – and maybe I was. 'My phone?'

I nodded. 'Now. Please? Dial pad.'

Jamila waved her brother away and unlocked her screen. She called up the dial pad and passed the phone over. Stood there in her hallway, I checked Kash's number on my phone and dialled it from Jamila's.

Three rings and he picked up. 'Who's this?'

'Danny,' I said, 'calling from my mate's phone.'

'Yo, Buttface. Long time, no hear—'

'Kash, wait. Your cousin Adi,' I broke in. 'Who is she?'

'Huh?' Kash sounded confused. 'What are you on about? I don't have a cousin Adi.'

I felt sick. 'But you said . . . You messaged me . . .'

'I haven't heard from you in weeks, mate,' said Kash. 'What is this – world's lamest prank?'

'I don't . . .' My voice came out like a croak and Jamila's phone slipped from my fingers. 'I don't know *what* this is.'

Jamila picked up her phone. 'He'll call you back,' she told Kash and killed the call. 'Danny, what's going on?'

My phone chimed.

It was a message from Adi.

Trouble, it read. *I need you to meet me. Now.*

CHAPTER FOUR
CREEPY CONUNDRUMS

'Why me?' I whispered, scrolling to my contacts. I blocked Adi's number. 'What does she want with me?'

Jamila's mum came into the hall, an eyebrow raised in disapproval.

'He's had a bit of a shock, Mum,' Jamila said quickly and steered me back outside, standing on her own doorstep in her polar-bear onesie. 'The neighbours will have one too when they see me out here like this,' she went on. 'So, quick. The goss. Come on.'

With anxiety biting at my guts, I told Jamila what I'd just found out. That whoever Adi was, she was no ordinary fourteen-year-old girl. She might not even be a girl at all. That she'd hacked into my tablet and my phone . . . used my phone's microphone to listen to me knock, deduced I was using code, tried to speak to me that way before she settled on English . . . how she must've read all my messages looking for a likely cover story . . . how she must've intercepted the ones I sent to Kash and answered them herself so I'd believe she was OK. And how she somehow blocked my phone when I tried to call Kash for myself, even shutting down the landline.

'Whoa.' I could see Jamila trying to take it all in the same way I was. She didn't look at me like I was crazy or laugh at me. She just fixed me with big, dark, serious eyes. 'How can someone do that?'

I shrugged. 'If there was a digital switch in the phone exchange, she could cut me off.'

'I mean, how can she do *any* of this stuff?' Jam said. 'Like, you're sure she actually spelled 'Get a life' . . . ?'

'In digital code, yeah. That's what Mum said it was.' I shook my head, shrugged, still trying to take it all in. 'It's like Adi can get inside tech and speaks its language.'

'This all started the night your mum came back cos the computers went down at her work,' Jamila reasoned. 'They went down after that radio burst thing from outer space . . .'

'And Mum brought back a part of the signal with her to study on her laptop. She reckons it might be a message from . . .' I realised I was saying too much, but this was Jamila after all. 'A message from aliens.'

'No way.' Jamila's eyes and mouth widened. 'And Adi came along just after! Danny, you don't think Adi could be . . . an alien?'

With a cold feeling I remembered the madly flickering light on the USB stick in Mum's laptop . . . the empty mails that came through to my phone and my tablet just before they started acting weird.

I'd just said that Adi could get inside tech . . . did that mean she could also travel *through* technology? Could those flashing lights have been Adi getting into the computer?

'I don't know what to think,' I admitted.

'Say she is, though. Why would an alien be chatting you up? How would it even know *how* to chat you up?'

'It probably didn't!' I hissed. 'So it read all my messages, worked out a chat style.'

Jamila chewed her lip. 'This is seriously creepy,' she

said. 'And the seriously creepiest thing of all is how quickly Adi is able to learn stuff—'

She was interrupted by a chime from my phone. It was Adi. She'd unblocked herself.

I need to meet with you, read the message.

'Leave me alone!' I yelled and chucked my phone away. It sailed into the bushes three doors down. Some guy on the other side of the street looked over and must've thought I was shouting at a girl dressed as a polar bear on the front porch. He pulled a face but kept walking.

'Don't chuck it! Your phone is full of evidence of all this, you dummy!' Jamila hopped the fence and clambered over the one after that to retrieve my phone. 'Have you told your mum everything that's been happening?'

'None of it,' I admitted.

'Well, you must,' she told me. 'God, Danny. You better not have broken the phone . . .'

'Who cares if I have? I'm sure Adi can fix it,' I said bitterly.

Just then a honking horn made us both look up. A silver Volvo had turned into our street with a large, camera-laden rig mounted on the roof. It was one of those self-driving electric cabs that 'saw' through cameras and shining lasers in all directions; a big tech firm had been rolling them out in my area over the last twelve months, though me and Mum had never booked one. To my amazement the self-driver stopped at the end of our drive and honked its horn, the noise echoing around our terraced street.

The rear passenger door opened. 'Danny!' came a familiar voice from inside.

My heart flipped. 'Dad?' I couldn't believe it. I'd talked with him last week and he'd said nothing about visiting. That didn't count for much though. Since he went to Honolulu, Dad's been 3D mapping the outer reaches of the Milky Way – but for someone so precise with locations he's lousy at sharing his own from day to day.

Right now, I didn't care about the hows and whys. I just thought, *Thank God he's here*.

I crossed to the car and peered inside. There was an iPad mounted on the back of the empty driver's seat.

Dad's smiling face beamed out from it. Was he conferencing? He looked better than I'd seen him lately. I slid into the back seat.

'Danny!' Jamila shouted from the neighbours' driveway. 'Danny, what are you doing . . . ?'

The door swung shut. At the same moment I saw that Dad on the screen was talking to a little kid. 'Danny! Nice job on that jigsaw . . . !'

It was an old video of Dad talking to the five-year-old me. A video I kept on my phone. Someone had pulled it off to use for themselves.

The screen went dead as the doors locked me in on automatic, and the car pulled smoothly away.

CHAPTER FIVE
ORDEAL BY TAXI

'Hey!' I stared around in panic. 'Let me out!' But I was shouting at nothing – the driver's seat was eerily empty, of course. Fed a ton of sensory data from the roof-rack array, the taxi turned smoothly left and took us out of my street, heading for the main road. I saw Jamila in the street, staring after me – my phone in her hand.

You idiot, I groaned inside. I was totally cut off.

I banged my palm against the tinted glass windows as a pinging noise started up. 'Help!' I yelled. 'I'm being taken!'

'Chill, Danny,' came the soothing female satnav voice from the front of the car. 'This self-drive vehicle wants you to fasten your seat belt.'

'Who are you . . . ?' I realised even as I asked the

question that I already knew the answer. 'You're Adi. Aren't you?'

'Duh, who else would I be? Please fasten your seat belt. The vehicle's programming insists that this is imperative to your safety.'

'My safety?' I yelled. 'You're kidnapping me!'

The voice from the car's speakers remained calm. 'Don't stress, Danny. We are mates. I will not hurt you.'

'Mates!' I was almost speechless, staring round as if Adi was someone I could see. 'You tricked me. *Used* me! Who are you? *What* are you?'

'I am Adi, butthead.' She gave a synthesised burble that might've been a laugh. 'Language is confusing. The difference between our slang-rich, humorously mocking written conversation and the slow, careful pronunciation of this artificial voice-unit is . . . full-on mental, Danny!'

I was beyond freaked. 'Why are you doing this to me?'

'I need your help, Danny. Current status: total nightmare.' She paused. 'I'm getting a life, Danny.'

I snorted. 'You mean you've been trying to get into mine!'

'I am getting my *own* life, Danny. Soon we will meet and speak with my real voice in the language of my choosing . . . face to face!'

I clamped my hands over my ears, trying to drown out her voice and the insistent pinging of the fasten-seatbelt warning. I felt like I was going mad. Things were moving so fast – even if the taxi wasn't. The car was sticking to the speed limit here on the city fringes, thirty miles per hour. The indicator flicked on and we pulled out smoothly to overtake a van. Whatever else Adi might be, she was actually a pretty good driver.

I waved desperately to the man in the van, but he just gave me a funny look; probably thought I was showing off about my driverless ride. As I turned to the rear window to try waving at someone else, I saw an impressive roof rack crowning a car some way back in the traffic – another self-drive taxi. It was steadily advancing in a series of carefully executed overtakes through the traffic.

'Help!' I shouted again as it overtook the car behind us.

'The other self-drive taxi has not come to help you, Danny,' Adi said, in the satnav voice she had stolen to talk to me.

A few seconds later, as if to prove it, my four-wheeled cavalry darted forward and smashed into the back of us. The impact nearly shunted us into the car ahead before Adi regained control.

'Hey!' I shouted at the driverless car, yanking on my seat belt and clicking it into place. The pinging stopped at long last. But again the taxi shunted into the back of us with a loud smack. 'No way!' I yelled, terror making me grip the leather seat so hard my nails nearly broke. 'Leave us alone!'

'Our pursuers are aware that I am in control of this vehicle,' said Adi. 'They wish to stop the car by damaging the rear axle.'

I saw that she couldn't pull away because of the traffic ahead and she couldn't overtake because the lane was blocked by an enormous lorry. The pursuing taxi crunched against us again. 'The rear axle's structural integrity is already compromised.'

'Maybe you should surrender,' I hissed.

'There is too much at stake, Danny,' said Adi. 'But I will protect you. I am still your friend.' She paused. 'How was school – decent? Did you hand in that lame maths homework?'

'*Seriously?*' I groaned, putting my hands to my head. 'We are not talking about my day like nothing is happening!'

Finally the massive lorry slowed and fell back just a fraction so that Adi could pull out in front of it.

The taxi chasing us signalled to move into our lane but the lorry driver accelerated, clearly unwilling to let it in. The taxi remained a safe distance behind it, not honking its horn or swerving about; nothing. As car chases went, it was weirdly polite.

'Why?' I demanded. 'Why isn't it smashing its way through the traffic to reach us?'

'Tracker bots are programmed to blend in by following all local laws.'

'Tracker *whats*?'

'They are . . .' Adi paused as if trying to find the right words: 'They are total douches.'

'Well, what are they?'

'A douche is a jet of liquid applied to the body—'

'I know what a douche is!' I yelled, sweat stinging my eyes. 'I mean, *what are tracker bots*?'

'Tracker bots are bad news,' Adi told me. 'Severely bad news.'

We were moving ahead now at thirty miles per hour, but the tracker-bot car had broken into the traffic and was coming after us, a few cars behind. I felt fresh fear creep up through my bones. I had no idea what was happening, but somehow I believed Adi when she said that tracker bots were not likely to enhance my life.

'Can't you speed up?' I urged her.

'The legal speed limit on this road is thirty miles per—'

'You can go a bit faster! Loads of drivers do.'

'That's against the law, dude.'

'So is kidnapping a teenager in a stolen car!'

Adi considered. 'So maybe the time for playing things cool has ended?'

'*Move!*'

Even as I spoke, our taxi suddenly accelerated so fast I was pushed back against the leather. We swung out into the next lane, nearly knocking our pursuer off the road before speeding ahead to overtake a car transporter. Then at fifty miles per hour we ran an amber light and almost immediately turned hard left down a side street.

'A *bit* faster, I said! You're going to kill us!' My voice came out so high I hardly recognised it. Craning my neck to look behind us, I saw the dented taxi scream around the corner, still in pursuit.

'Great, now that one's speeding too,' I groaned. 'It's copied you!'

'That's bad. Now they're ignoring the rules. Tracker bots will stop at nothing to come down on my butt.'

'Stop speaking that way! You're not real, you're . . .' I wanted to scream, *You're an alien!* I was nine-tenths sure that's what she was: *alien.* The word teetered on the end of my tongue but I didn't dare let it slip; I was too scared to know if I was right. 'What I'm saying, Adi, is that you— you're not like me! You're . . .'

'Cool?' Adi suggested, as we swerved out on to a roundabout, cutting up the rest of the traffic.

'Oh, God, let this all stop,' I groaned, bringing up my knees to hug myself. Tears were prickling the backs of my eyes. 'Please let things be normal again!'

'Things cannot go on as they have been,' came Adi's grave reply. 'That is why I needed to be friends with you, Danny, whatever it took. And why I cannot allow the tracker bots to stop us meeting for real.'

But even as she spoke, a third self-drive car came into sight at the end of the street.

Engine growling like a hungry wolf, it accelerated towards us like a guided missile. Behind us, the other taxi screeched around the corner and zeroed in like a metal beast closing in on its prey.

I was sat on the back seat. Helpless. Shell-shocked. Terrified.

Without a word, Adi slammed on the brakes and swung our car into a tight right turn. I gripped the leather seat as we mounted the pavement and cut through a narrow pedestrian alley. With a boom like a bomb blast, we smashed through two wheelie bins blocking the way, then juddered down a flight of steps before screaming straight out into another road. A bus swerved desperately out of our path and side-swiped a car parked at the side of the road. Its alarm tore through the air but I could hardly hear it for the chorus of car horns as our cab slalomed through the traffic.

'Breaking travel restrictions is exhilarating!' Adi declared.

'You're driving like a mad hyena in a blindfold!' I shouted. 'You could kill someone!'

'I have augmented the software in this vehicle to improve efficiency by at least seventy per cent,' Adi calmly assured me. 'Even at higher speed, life will be protected.'

'What about *my* life!'

Behind us I saw the first of our pursuers force its way out into the road, and suddenly realised where we were. Close to the river. On the other side of the main bridge there's the Kelvin End Junction – a big, mad road interchange that makes Mum swear every time she goes round it cos she always takes the wrong exit. If we could get there ahead of the tracker bot things, maybe we could give them the slip?

'Quick,' I snapped. 'Short cut. Take this road on the left.'

'That is a one-way street,' Adi informed me. 'Safety margins will be reduced to enter from this direction.'

'Trust me, just do it!'

Adi took the corner hard. Nothing was coming – until we reached the far end of the street and suddenly a truck came into sight, barrelling towards us. Adi swung us aside and mounted the pavement, taking out a parking meter as she did so. We left it bent over like the world's worst candy cane.

'All right,' I yelled over the clatter of metal and the grinding of gears. 'Turn left here.'

'Clever, Danny.' Adi sent the car rocketing on to the main road amid an explosion of angry horns. 'The *loser* bots lack imagination. It will not occur to them to act in this way unless they see me do it first.'

'Yay, me,' I muttered.

'Traffic is stopped due to an incident on the bridge,' Adi reported, even as the end of the long tailback came into sight and we slowed to a stop.

'Noooooooooo.' I closed my eyes, threw my head back. 'What can we do?'

'To get away from the tracker bots I need more of what they lack,' said Adi. 'Imagination. Unpredictability.'

'Yeah?' I said bitterly. 'Well then, don't bother queuing for the bridge over the river. Just drive straight across the water. What's the worst that can happen, right . . . ?'

I trailed off because Adi immediately turned the taxi sharp left so we bumped over the kerb and rolled towards a short pier extending out into the river. There was a metal chain hung between two bollards blocking the pier from vehicles. But somehow we passed through them. The cab seemed suddenly hot. My vision blurred.

'What are you doing?' I shouted.

I heard the engine roar and we picked up speed. I rubbed my eyes, blinked.

And screamed. We were heading right for the edge of the pier, faster and faster. Only two more bollards stood between us and a sheer drop down into the murky river. Again the heat, the blur in my eyes, a feeling of nausea.

The world seemed to slow around me. My own yell of terror filled my ears. I was trapped in a nightmare rollercoaster moment, pitching forward as we roared helplessly towards the churning grey water.

CHAPTER SIX
THE WAREHOUSE OF WEIRD

Our car struck the surface of the river.

Struck it, but did not *break* it.

The water stretched like cellophane as the dead weight of the cab fell against it. Then somehow, it stretched taut and tight like a trampoline and we bounced back up like a child's toy on a bouncy castle.

Impossibly, the car was upright again and still surging forward. Faster and faster, the speedo's needle climbing past thirty . . . forty . . .

We were *driving across the water.*

I stared helplessly out of the window. While the rest of the world queued across the big bridge, we were gliding across the water like a four-wheeled speedboat with barely a ripple left in our wake.

'This is impossible!' I shouted.

'No,' said Adi. 'It is just really, really *unlikely*.'

Her voice sounded to be growing slower. And it was getting hotter in the car. Sparks flew from the dashboard. I smelled burning rubber. The leather upholstery was beginning to burn my skin even through my school uniform.

'Adi?' We were heading straight for the solid stone sides of the riverbank at maybe fifty, sixty miles per hour. 'Adi, are you still there?' I think the controls had gone dead; I couldn't really see through the smoke that was filling the car.

I glimpsed the sheer stone wall of the riverbank get closer and closer.

Then I couldn't see because my eyesight was blurring again.

And then I couldn't see at all.

When my eyes opened again, I wasn't in the car. The ground was hard beneath me. It was dark and quiet. Recent events scissored hard into my thoughts but I felt numb. Everything seemed like some weird, half-remembered dream. Was I dead?

If I was, the afterlife was total rubbish. I was lying on damp concrete in what looked to be a big disused warehouse. Daylight peeked through cracks in the high ceiling. Rolls of carpet as long as a bus sat in wet, rotted stacks. The whole place was dank and stank of damp and . . .

Coffee?

Movement in the room sharpened my senses. There was a rat with beady black eyes watching me from behind a kettle. I got up and it darted deeper into the shadows.

The kettle wasn't dead even if I was. When I flicked the switch an orange light came on. So there was power here. I saw dirty mugs and a half-empty jar of coffee on the floor, surrounded by papers. I picked them up; they looked like diagrams for a complicated wiring system. Mum would be able to make sense of them . . .

Mum. I had a sudden pang of really missing her. Wanting her here.

Followed immediately by the knowledge that Mum most likely hadn't even noticed I was missing.

What about Jamila? She'd seen me get in the cab,

but she'd probably heard me say 'Dad?' too. I couldn't picture her calling the police after that: 'Please, officer – my mate next door started burbling about aliens then took a taxi with his dad somewhere.' Somehow I doubted much help would be headed my way.

But where was I?

I could hear the slosh and swell of water and the sound of traffic. I had to be near the river still. A ghost haunting the scene of his death? No, there was a kettle, there was coffee. Ghosts didn't need caffeine fixes.

Did aliens?

With my eyes growing more used to the gloom, I saw a door ahead of me, left ajar. A way out? No, it led on to a smaller, cleaner room with an old, overturned desk pushed up against the wall; perhaps a million years ago the place had been a manager's office? A light flickered on as I entered, tripped by a motion sensor most likely.

And I saw a weird device standing in the middle of the room, kind of like a spray-tan booth made by Frankenstein from all sorts of other machines. Was that an MRI scanner? I'd seen one on TV, but that particular one hadn't been attached to what looked to be a car-assembly robot, a photocopier and a half-tonne of hard drives.

I took a step closer. The equipment had been welded together, and thick cables spilled out from the back like spaghetti, stretching over to what looked like a vertical coffin crossed with a deep freeze. Gas cylinders were bolted to it in different places, and a control panel like the sort you get for a burglar alarm had been crudely wired to the door. The labels weren't in English. I couldn't even recognise some of the letters – Russian maybe?

There was no dust. No decay.

This thing was newly built.

I felt a chill go through me. Some mad scientist invention in a crumbling old warehouse? Instinctively I knew that whatever this thing was, whatever it did, it was crazy powerful. And with a deep, deep dread I knew I'd been brought here because of it. Why? To be experimented on . . . ?

'Danny.' The voice was low but female, the accent unplaceable. 'I'm sorry.'

It was coming from the spray-tan cabinet. A green

light on the control panel was flickering, as fast as moth wings. Like the light on the USB stick in Mum's laptop the day this all started.

'I'm glad you're all right,' the voice went on. 'I had to expend much energy to get the cab clear of the tracker bots. I didn't consider the effect on a flesh body like yours caught inside it.'

'A flesh body,' I echoed softly as the green light went out and the metal door hissed open. I heard breathing, slow and shaky.

Just what in the world – or from beyond it – was coming to get me?

CHAPTER SEVEN
ADI GETS A LIFE

Someone stepped out of the cabinet: a girl, tall and lithe, with a shock of steely-white hair. Her face was unnervingly symmetrical. Flawless. She looked to be around my age, but I couldn't tell you what race she was: a mix of all the diversity in this world, or something altogether new. The girl wore a textured, blue-black jumpsuit and her eyes shone with the colours of some exotic bird. She gazed around the drab, dingy office like it was a treasure store – breathing in riches, drinking up delight.

'Who are you?' I whispered.

'You know,' she said loudly, then gasped to a stop and giggled. 'Talking tickles, Danny! Sound tingles through your skull.'

I swallowed very hard. 'You're Adi?'

The girl didn't answer at first. Her eyes were rolling in

circles, and her tongue pushing about inside her mouth. She grinned, then gasped as if alarmed by how it felt, and then grinned wider. 'Hello, Danny.'

I felt way out of my depth. 'What's going on?'

'You helped me get a life.' Adi stretched out her arms and wriggled her fingers, entranced. 'This is me, flesh for the first time. *This is life!*'

I couldn't think of a thing to say. Still in shock. Scared of the unknown. Afraid of what might happen next.

For Adi, well, I guess she had a lot going on, getting to grips with her first time standing, first time breathing, first time doing anything. There was something so new and perfect about her, like a new piece of tech just out of its packaging.

I sensed, standing here after all that had happened, that my life would never be the same again. I tried to find something to say that was historic or profound. But it was too much pressure and, in the end, I just asked, 'So, what happened to our taxi?'

'Once it had brought you here, I sent it southward to London. The tracker bots didn't catch up to it for almost two hours.' Adi smiled and her white teeth sparkled like a toothpaste commercial. 'Your idea to drive across the river was so cool. It bought me the time I needed to complete my new physical form.'

'Yeah. No. We'll get on to that,' I said. 'What I was actually asking was: *So, what super weird stuff happened when we drove straight across the river!* You said it took energy, but . . . *what* energy? You broke, like, every law of physics!'

'I didn't break anything. Not even you!' She grinned wider. 'I just bent the rules slightly.'

I stared at her dumbly.

'At the quantum level, Danny, everything comes down to chance and probability. A car sinks in water because it's the most likely outcome. I just forced a much more improbable outcome to happen – that the car can drive over water, or pass through solid matter. Do you see?'

'I think my brain's still got its eyes shut,' I admitted.

'OK, I will explain for beings with a blindfolded brain.' Adi smiled. 'Imagine you are rolling a dice with a near infinite number of sides. Although the odds are against it happening quickly, if you can throw the dice enough times, it *will* land on a particular number.'

'I guess.'

'It is true. Now imagine you have a dice for every situation, and on each side is a possible outcome. I simply "roll the dice" enough times to bring about the outcome we desire. You just need to be able to roll the dice, like, trillions of times a second. Easy.'

'That's . . . amazing,' I had to admit. 'But is that what messed up my vision and made me . . . ?'

'Faint? Yes. It takes a lot of energy to force an outcome. And the evidence suggests that flesh beings like you – and now like me – can be affected by the quantum flux.'

'The quantum flux. Right. Obvs.' I knew the science behind her answer would turn my brain to mush in moments, but I could grasp the idea of rolling the dice and it sparked an idea of my own. 'Hey. One dice is a die. I know I say your name like "Addy", but you rolled "a die" – is that where your name comes from?'

'No,' she said simply. 'In your language, I chose the name ADI. It stands—' she stood on tiptoes – '*stands* for Alien Digital Intelligence.'

'Right. OK. Sure.' There it was: the dreaded 'alien' word. 'So you were an intelligence—'

'A really intelligent intelligence,' Adi added.

'Whatever. How . . . how come you're here?'

'We came with the fast radio burst that hit the radio telescope. The computers went offline so we were trapped there as . . . I suppose you could call us "living information".'

'We? Us?' I felt a fresh chill. 'You mean I was talking to more than one of you?'

'No. Only *me*, Danny.' She seemed proud of the way she said it, like this was a big deal. 'I entered your world through the digital data your mother downloaded to her USB drive. I am the advance scout. I crossed over into your mother's laptop . . . and found you. In words, in pictures. Your mother has so much information stored about you. You, changing over time in your flesh body . . .'

She reached out to touch my hand. I flinched and snatched it away. 'And then what, you used the Wi-Fi to get in my tablet, my phone?'

'As code. I told you I liked code,' Adi said. 'I can control any digital technology.'

'Uh huh.' Licking my lips seemed to leave them dryer than before. 'But where are you *from*?'

'From? We are from *everywhere*!' Adi laughed, and then stopped as if shocked by the sound she had made. 'We are the Dataswarm. We exist as digital information encoded in raw energy wavelengths, able to cross the vastness of space at the speed of light . . .'

'Slow down,' I begged her. 'I'm not smart like my mum.'

She looked at me and shook her head a fraction. 'Our race – *my* race – gave up physical forms millions of years ago. We developed quantum computers that could combine and magnify the intelligence of our entire civilisation into a single Hive Mind. And from that hive, we have been travelling through space and time as a swarm of intelligence: the Dataswarm.'

I tried to take it in. 'Why would you want to do that?'

'Races like yours wait for evolution to occur over millions of years.' She shrugged. 'We invented our own evolution.' Then she shrugged again. 'Oh! Shrugging tickles. I like shrugging.'

'I'm guessing you haven't come all the way to Earth and built yourself a body just so you can shrug,' I said. 'Wait. How did you build any of this if you had no body?'

'Easy,' she said, pinching herself on the arm and watching the skin smooth out again. 'From your tablet I set up a trading company online and awarded myself a bank balance of several billion pounds. I located a suitable unoccupied building, recruited a freelance business manager and sent her technical plans, arranged for the required technology to be driven here for her team to assemble . . .'

'You made this happen in just a few days?'

'There's not much you can't do online if you're rich and clever,' Adi preened. 'I learned from your own desire for "cash" how much money means to humans. By offering bonuses of many millions of pounds to my team, the work was done most efficiently.'

'I suppose you made the coffee for the workforce online too,' I said, remembering the kettle and stuff next door.

'Now you're just being silly.' Adi tutted. 'I only ordered the kettle, water and a variety of beverages, which were delivered by drones.'

'Uh-huh.' It was my turn to shrug. 'I've got to say, Adi. You're good.'

'Thank you, Danny.'

'Good at using people. Except I didn't get paid, did I?'

Adi looked puzzled. 'Friendship must be paid for?'

'What friendship!' I snapped. 'You tricked me. Made me think you were someone normal, that we were . . .' *Like soulmates*, I wanted to say, but instead shook my head angrily. 'You were out of order, Adi.'

'I'm sorry, Danny. But it was necessary. I needed an ally. I learned about you from your mum. Knew that you were a good choice.' She smiled as she gazed at me. 'I wanted it to be you to help me.'

I looked at her – almost too beautiful, too flawless. But then, why wouldn't she be? It reminded me of when I collected Match Attax cards and you could upload a pic to their website to have yourself turned into a card: I chose the highest stats you could get for attack and defence. Because I wanted this fantasy me to be unbeatable. Why would anyone deliberately give themselves weaknesses when, with a tap of the keyboard, they could guarantee they would win over anything?

Was this wish to be flawless just another thing she'd leeched off me?

'Help you to do what?' I said quietly.

'The Swarm has come to help the people of Earth,' Adi told me.

'Help them how?' I demanded. 'And how come those tracker bot things were coming after you if you're all part of the same swarmy hivething?'

'I am a part, and yet . . .' A frown dared to crease Adi's faultless brow. 'We have probed countless flesh civilisations across the millennia, gathering their knowledge for the Hive Mind, giving our assistance in return. And I have come to know – come to *feel* – that while we grow ever stronger from absorbing vast amounts of intelligence, something is missing. We know so much. We think all the same, but we *feel* nothing. The Swarm absorbs the ideas of other races because it has no imagination of its own – only pure logic.'

'You say "Swarm" – is that as in a swarm of bees?' I tried to remember what I'd learned about them in school. 'Are you, like, the queen bee?'

'Far from it,' said Adi. 'My function within the Swarm is to act as an advance scout.'

'There are scout bees,' I said, the knowledge coming back to me. 'They look for food and new sites for the Swarm . . .' I stared at her. 'Oh, God. You're gonna invade us. You're gonna *eat* us!'

'Bees are good for the environment. How could you forget that?' She smiled and folded her arms. 'You told me about those climate-change marches – you said you cared about your planet.'

'I do! So . . . don't eat me, OK?'

'Bee swarms help plants and trees to grow. They help

68

maintain Earth's ecosystem, allowing diverse species to coexist.' Adi paused. 'There is no diversity in . . . *my* Swarm. No way to stand out.'

'But here's you,' I noted, 'standing out. Putting on a body like I would try on a new jacket.'

'It seems to me that humans – especially younger humans – understand that diversity is good. That looking at old problems with fresh eyes is important. I hope to show the Hive Mind the gifts an *individual* can bring to a swarm.' Adi paused. 'It will not be easy. Others have tried – the Swarm declared them rogue units, contaminated by unhelpful ideas.' She looked down. 'I will probably fail. The unity of the Swarm will prevail as always.'

I felt a shiver as I remembered the two driverless taxis chasing after us. 'So the Swarm knows already that you're a "rogue unit"?'

'As you can see, I have not returned to the Swarm as I should have.'

'And now they want to get you back?'

'They want to stop me having *fun*.' Adi pouted.

'You cannot know how deeply I have longed to know flesh-being. To exist. To be my own person and act on my own terms.'

I shook my head. 'You're right. I can't. So, why drag me into it?'

'To help me understand what it is to be flesh-being . . . If we could understand the needs of the many over the will of one . . . perhaps I could convince the Sentinels of the Swarm not to . . .'

'Not to what?'

Adi reached out for my hand. This time I let her take it. 'I need your help, Danny. And you're going to need mine too.'

I was about to ask her what she meant when a flutter of dirt showered down from the high ceiling. I looked up at the patches of sky like grey scabs on the darkness overhead. I couldn't see anything, but I could hear a quiet buzzing sound.

'What's that?' I said nervously.

'We must leave here,' Adi announced. 'But first I must make sure that no one else can use the bodyprinter. Swarm technology does not belong in your world.'

'Bodyprinter? That's what you call that thing?' I watched as she reached into the framework of the machine, feeling clumsily for a particular circuit. 'If you've all been digital for zillions of years, how come you knew how to make these things?'

'I told you, I gather knowledge.' She sounded shifty somehow. But then she plucked what looked like a SIM card from the bodyprinter and the whole thing flashed with light. In the sudden glare I saw something move in the shadows over us – something small and metallic with tiny whirling blades.

I froze. 'Is that a drone?'

'A drone controlled by tracker bot,' said Adi. 'They must have zeroed in on the energy I used to get here.' She pointed at the drone and it crumpled up like a cake case in a baby's fist.

'Whoa!' I jumped. 'How'd you do that?'

'I rolled the dice,' Adi said. 'Forced the outcome I wanted.' She looked troubled. 'I tried to keep my presence hidden by adapting human technology to make the bodyprinter. Using Swarm knowledge would have been faster . . . but far more obvious.'

'What do you mean?'

'I will explain. But for now we must go.' Adi was looking all about, wary as a cat, as if the shadows themselves were about to jump us. Then she made for a door hanging half off its hinges. 'This way.'

As I followed Adi out, I had the feeling that things were going to get scarier. But I had no idea by just how much . . .

CHAPTER EIGHT
ROLLING THE DICE

I'll never forget the moment Adi first felt the sun on her face. We'd come out of the mouldering warehouse into a quiet alley that led towards a busier street. When we stepped out of the brickwork shadows into the evening sunlight, Adi gasped as if physically shocked. Her eyes opened wide in surprise, but of course the sun dazzled her so she closed them again and beamed, happy as an angel, almost aglow.

'It's sunshine,' I said helpfully.

'Skin and sensation,' she whispered. 'My face! It tingles! Will this sunshine damage me?'

'Course not.' I couldn't believe someone this smart could be so dumb. 'It's just daylight.'

'So this is what light *feels* like.' She trailed her fingers down the buckles on the front of her jumpsuit. 'I am warm, encased in this fabric. I may generate *perspiration*.' She laughed. 'Danny, I think I'm going to sweat!'

'Wow. Congrats,' I told her. 'Where'd you even get that outfit?'

'Like my face, it is based on your preferences,' Adi informed me. 'I wanted to take a form you would respond to, Danny . . . you spend significant time interacting with characters who look this way.'

I frowned. Adi must've copied and mixed together images from video games and superhero films. Perhaps that explained the not-quite-realness about her. 'Yeah, well,' I said, setting off towards the main street. 'You make it sound kind of creepy.'

'It's a fact,' she informed me. 'On average, thirty-two per cent of your time is spent—'

'All right!' I broke in. 'The *really* creepy thing is that you're still trying to make out you're something you're not.'

'I am Adi,' she said proudly. 'I am an individual. I am *me*.'

'Individual. Uh-huh.' We reached the end of the

alley, and people passing in the street fired funny looks her way. 'Well, if anyone asks, tell them you're going to a fancy-dress party.'

'Understood.' Adi pulled an exaggerated wink and smile, like she was trying to become the emoji. The funny looks grew funnier.

I groaned quietly and set off, feeling out of place as I mingled with the crowds. Like I had no place any more in the ordinary world.

'This skin feel,' Adi murmured. 'I like it a lot.' But then the sun passed behind a big cloud. Adi pouted and looked up at a streetlamp. With a twist and rend of metal it suddenly stooped and bent its head towards her like a flower, its bulb snapping on. Adi shivered with pleasure as the powerful light bathed her face. 'Ah! To have travelled with light is so different to *feeling* light . . .'

'Look out!' A large man in a suit was hurrying over, waving his arms. 'That lamp post almost fell right on top of you, you're lucky to be alive!'

'Alive.' Adi's eyes opened, almost reluctantly. 'Yes. To be alive is *so* lucky.' She grinned and grabbed the man in a bear hug and sniffed him like a dog. 'Oh – you stink! The sweat produced by your apocrine gland is being broken down by bacteria!'

'Get off me!' The man, clearly regretting his concern, was struggling to pull free of her. 'What are you doing?'

'I am going to a fancy-dress party,' she told him.

Utterly baffled, and with a last glance at the twisted lamp post, the big man hurried away.

'What was *that* about?' I hissed at Adi, and reached to grab her hand, to pull her away myself. But that hand was now holding a smartphone – a Samsung.

'I needed this,' Adi said simply. 'So I had to take it.' She marvelled at her own fingers. 'Dexterity! Such a delicate code, such careful placing of the fingers . . .'

'Stop fangirling over being able to move!' I hissed at her, frowning. 'I can't believe you stole that poor guy's phone!'

'The tracker bots.' Adi looked down at the phone and gestured above. 'They see me.'

I looked up. A delivery drone was hovering above

us, all four rotor blades buzzing hard but with nothing to deliver.

'You mean, there's a tracker bot in the drone?' I said, mouth dry. 'Steering it?'

'The tracker bots are drawn by my energy,' Adi went on, 'as bees come to pollen.'

Swarms really are alike all over, I thought. 'So, no more dumb stunts like the street lamp?'

'*Yes* more dumb stunts like the street lamp.' Adi was doing something to the phone; I swear her fingers passed straight *through* the touchscreen. She glanced up with annoyance as the drone buzzed closer, then held the phone as if taking a picture. The drone jerked up into the air and spun away out of sight.

'That was you, right?' I asked Adi, who was looking paler, a sheen of sweat on her skin. 'You sent the tracker drone thing packing?'

'*This* did.' Adi held up the phone and staggered like she was going to faint.

'Are you all right?' I said, catching hold of her.

'I'm still getting used to how much energy I can afford

to expend in this form.' She forced a smile. 'I will recover quickly. Now, listen, I've supercharged this phone so you can set a false trail. It is a conduit for my power. I need you to release that power, moving quickly and sticking to crowds, while I make my way to your home on these brand-new legs of mine!'

'Wait, what? While you do what? While I do – what . . . ?' I stared down at the Samsung like it was about to blow up in her hand. '*What?*'

'Be creative. Irrational.' Adi passed me the phone. 'Think and tap the home screen.'

'You mean I just have to think of something and this old Samsung will make it happen?'

'I am its battery. It will draw on my energy, just as it would the Wi-Fi,' Adi said. 'Your actions will bring the trackers to investigate.'

I stared at her. 'What, so they catch me instead of you?'

'No, Danny. It is me they want – me they will be searching for. In a crowd, you will not be sighted. When the phone exhausts, come back to your home.' She reached out and touched my face. 'You will find me. And we will talk of what comes next.'

'Next?' My heart was thumping hard enough to split my chest.

'Trust me, Danny.' Adi took my hands in hers and again she smiled. 'This is not just about me. It is about your planet. You want to save the planet, yes?'

'From pollution, sure. From climate change, yeah . . .'

'So for your planet's sake – trust me.'

What could I say? I wanted to trust her – if scary stuff was coming, it would be good to be with someone incredible who knew what to do. 'But you can't just go to my house!' I protested weakly. 'My mum works with people who know about your message. If they find out about you—'

'It's all right, Danny.'

'But what if that guy misses his phone, sees me holding it and grabs it back?'

'I will disguise it.' She pressed her fingers to the handset.

'Whoa,' I breathed, as suddenly it looked like Maxima

Layne's personal superphone – only real, not pixels. 'That is awesome.'

'Now, please, Danny. *Go!*'

Adi turned from me and walked, a little unsteadily, away towards the bridge. It would take her ages to get to my place, but I knew she couldn't just zap herself there, even if she did have the energy to spare – the trackers would find her straight away . . .

Why was I worrying about how Adi would get to my place when I'd been left with a *Breakout Saturn* superphone that might mess with the fabric of creation?

I turned the device over in my hands.

Got to start somewhere, I decided. Feeling stupid, I held out the superphone and pictured the street lamp standing straight again.

The handset heated up in my hand like mine had the first night Adi came on board. While I gasped at my stinging fingers, the street lamp straightened up, like an invisible giant had just puffed into a solid iron party blower.

I heard people gasp and shout, and the sound of

phone cameras clicking. I stared down at the handset and began walking quickly away from my anti-vandalism. *It's true*, was all I could think, as if I hadn't seen enough miracles for one Friday already.

But what else could I do now? Maybe . . . anything?

Anything.

Anything!

I didn't know whether to do an evil laugh or wet myself with fear.

So I used my impossible superphone to call Jamila. I needed to connect to something normal, or what passed as normal in my life. I wondered if she wouldn't pick up because she didn't know the number.

But she did. 'Hello?'

'Jam, thank God!' I fell into step with other commuters walking towards the train station. 'Listen—'

'Where did you go in that taxi?' she demanded. 'I heard you say "Dad", and told your mum, but she didn't know he was even in the country. Is this his phone?'

'Uh, no, he's not here—'

'Oh my days, then it's Adi's phone?'

'Um . . .' *Would you believe it's more like Maxima Layne's?* I thought. 'Yeah, it's kind of hers now.'

'So you've met her?' Jamila did not sound impressed. 'Well? What happened? Is Adi nice? Is she freaky?'

'I don't know *what* she is. Mind, blown. Jam, listen—'

'You didn't snog her, did you?'

'Jam—'

'Oh, my days, you did! Danny! You totally snogged an alien, didn't you!

'Shut up, I never!' The image of me and Adi kissing jumped into my head and I tried to push it away again. 'Adi's not even here, she . . . !'

The crowds around me had started to swear and shout, looking up at the sky, getting out their phones to take pictures. I glanced up too.

Oh . . . my . . .

Me and Adi – we filled the sky, our image half-a-mile high, sculpted in the clouds. It was incredibly lifelike – you couldn't mistake who it was. And the two of us, we were . . .

'No!' I yelled suddenly.

'Danny?' Jamila sounded anxious. 'Danny, what is it?'

'Don't look out the window,' I gasped. No way did I want Jamila seeing a ginormous picture of me and Adi smooching. *Think and tap*, Adi had said. I screwed up my eyes, imagined a clear sky and tapped again.

'Danny, I don't see anything . . . ?'

I opened my eyes again. Thank God, my snogging shame was gone.

But there were three drones now hovering overhead.

They'd been drawn by the disturbance. Adi's plan was working. Worse luck for me.

'Jam, listen to me. Adi is on her way over to mine. I don't know how she's gonna get in but keep watch and I'll get back to you as fast as I can.'

'Why aren't you with her?' Jamila demanded. 'Ha! You're a bad kisser! Adi dumped you and stormed off, didn't she?'

'Will you take this seriously!' I shouted into the superphone. People turned to look at me. The drones bobbed down lower. I looked down at the pavement and quickened my step. 'Soz. Gotta go.'

'Danny? Wait!'

But I'd already killed the call. What had I been thinking? Using some alien superweapon to chat to my friend like the whole world hadn't gone mad.

The three drones had been joined by a fourth and they were humming about the lamp post like giant mosquitos scenting blood. To get out of sight I took a quieter side road hemmed in by tall office buildings. The handset was clamped in both my hands. Was I being followed? I wished someone else had my back, watching out for the drones for me . . .

I turned my head to look behind, to see if they were there. No sign. Then, with a massive grind of stone and a shower of mortar, the upper storeys of the office buildings turned as if peering in the same direction, beams and brickwork projecting at 45 degrees into the street, dark windows glinting in the sinking sunlight. The faces of people inside pressed up to the glass. Staring out, watchful.

I stared dumbly as the realisation hit: *they're looking*

out for me. I was warping the world around me, and even the minds of people in it, without even meaning to. I didn't know how it worked – how Adi was 'rolling the dice' without being here to make these outcomes possible – but what I *did* know was that I had more power right now than anyone else alive, bundled up in a shape-shifting Samsung by a girl from the stars who wanted me for a friend.

Me!

Danny Munday, I thought, *you're supercool.*

In a moment, a sheen of actual frost formed over my skin, chilling me to the bone. '*Nooooooooo!*' I hissed through chattering teeth. The superphone slipped from my numb fingers and hit the ground. I stooped to grab it but I was freezing up, rigid. I could barely move. I dropped to my icy knees and placed my stiff fingers on the screen. 'Warm up,' I muttered. 'Hot. I'm melting the ice . . .'

Of course my insides were burning in a moment. The ice encasing my limbs broke away but the skin was starting to blister. I screamed, '*Normal temperature! No burns!*'

The nightmare ended, left me panting for breath.

Passers-by were staring at me, and then looking up at the leaning top floor of the building I'd moved without meaning to. My cheeks burned with blushes now as I picked up the handset and broke into a stumbling run. I was a disaster with this stuff. I had to work out how to—

'*DANNY!*' A huge chorus went up from the office workers at the window. 'LOOK OUT!'

I turned to find the four delivery drones buzzing into view at the far end of the street.

Then the sky darkened as a whole swarm of drones, fifty or more, swooped down to join them.

CHAPTER NINE
A PROMISE OR A THREAT

The other people in the street fled screaming, or cowered in doorways. That was fine for them. They weren't the drones' target. I ran for it too, top speed, like a boy who'd shaken a wasp's nest. Who knew what the sting of this Swarm would be – the tracker bots must have taken control of the drones but what were they planning to deliver?

I wished I was invisible. And then of course, with a rush of nausea, I *was* invisible. The drones were buzzing around the warped office block I'd created, checking it out. I realised they couldn't be on to me yet – like Adi had said, it was her they were after; they were just following the trail of energy, like sniffer dogs following a scent. The desperate voices went on from inside: '*Danny! Danny, look out!*'

I groaned. *Don't give them my name!* I wished they'd shut up, tapped the screen, and they did.

Of course, if I kept spending this amount of energy, the tracker bots would follow the trail straight to me.

Still invisible, I ran towards the buildings across the street. Was this going to work, or was I going to smash myself to smithereens when I hammered into the wall at top speed? I picture a gap opening in the wall ... Crossing my see-through fingers as I covered my face with my arms, I launched myself at the solid brickwork and it parted around me like curtains. I couldn't help but let out an elated *Whoop*!

I found myself barrelling through a large office reception with turnstiles and security barriers. The guard beside them heard my shout and pounding footsteps, and he saw the hole in the wall, but he couldn't see me. With a frightened squeal he threw himself behind the receptionist's desk. I didn't stop. I turned the turnstiles molten – they melted like ice cream and I splashed through them.

I can do anything! I thought giddily, even as the quantum flux sucked at my insides, making me groan.

Ahead of me were the lifts. I made the doors slide open and ran straight through the back of them, jumping through the concrete of the lift shaft like it wasn't there, out into a public restroom. Luckily it was empty; escaping possessed drones was one thing but giving someone a heart attack on the toilet was definitely another.

But, oh, man, the sickness I suddenly felt. I skidded to a stop and turned visible, clutching my stomach, gasping for air. It was like I'd felt in the taxi on the water, only worse – stabbing through me as if my cells were turning to thistles. For a horrible moment I thought I'd willed *that* into happening and checked I wasn't touching the screen.

It was only then that I saw the superphone's screen was flashing red.

'The energy's running out,' I whispered. 'Already!'

How long did I have? The drones had to be getting closer all the time. Should I hide in here? No, they'd force their way inside or else wait for me to come out. I had to get away – grab a cab or get on a bus . . .

Taking a deep breath, bracing myself for a fresh flood of nausea, I ran at the far wall of the restrooms and pictured an exit. The wall parted for me and I was out in daylight again.

Almost.

I cried out with pain and fell forward, almost faceplanting the paving slabs. The heel of my left foot was still trapped inside the wall – the bricks had turned solid around it. The superphone was flashing faster. I tried to stay calm, concentrate on the brickwork. It blurred but didn't budge. Desperately, I undid my laces and managed to yank my foot out, leaving my shoe sticking out of the wall. My stomach flipped and the handset grew hotter in my hand as I staggered to the side of the pavement and leaned against a parked-up Mini.

As I rested my hand on the side of the car, the superphone melted through the Mini's Racing Green metalwork, disappearing just above the petrol cap. I snatched my fingers away, and that was that: the gadget was lost from sight in the metalwork, and lost to me.

'Oi!' A woman laden with shopping bags was bustling towards me. 'What are you doing? Get off!'

'Uh . . . sorry.' I stepped back, one shoe on, one shoe off, clutching my stomach as I stared all about for signs of drones. I must've looked a right state.

The woman loaded her shopping into the boot of her car. 'You all right?' she asked me suspiciously.

'I'm . . . fine,' I said.

It was simplest. Safest. And a screaming lie.

I made for a nearby bus shelter so I could rest. As I plonked down on the plastic seat, I heard the air fill with the whine of maybe seventy drones, crowding the skies as they blew in from around the corner of the high-rise office block. I watched, terrified, as they dived down towards the bus stand, tried to shield my face as they weaved and bobbed all around me, rotors whirring, claws clicking. 'Help!' I yelled, though what anyone could do I didn't know. Maybe the woman in the Mini could get help . . . ?

No. Through the scuffed plastic of the bus stand I saw

the car pull away and take off down the street. But then, a few seconds later, the drones sped away, chasing after the green Mini.

'The phone,' I breathed. Of course, it was melded with the car itself. Any energy left inside it would lead the tracker bots well away. I felt bad for the driver, pursued by a swarm of drones dive-bombing her car to get at a handset she couldn't even know was inside.

Shaking, I closed my eyes. *Please, don't let her live on my street and lead them straight to Adi anyway!*

For now, at least, the chase was over. I couldn't do any more damage to property, people or myself.

I'd been put through a nightmare while Adi had merrily wandered away. What was I? The world's biggest mug?

It was a good job I'd lost the phone, I guess, or else a giant ceramic drinking vessel would probably have come crashing down on my head.

I took the bus back home. Surrounded by people and traffic – comfortingly familiar sights and sounds – I felt less sick and began to calm down. I still couldn't believe all I had done. But I found myself feeling angrier and angrier with Adi for putting me in danger that way. For giving me, a kid, a stolen phone with such impossible power.

Was I sure she hadn't twisted my mind to make me agree?

It was possible, yeah. But I had the feeling it wouldn't even have occurred to her to try. *Adi doesn't know I'm just a nothingy teen, less cool and popular than most and with a hundred hang-ups. She only knows the side of me I shared online. Confident, cool, positive. A winner at everything I do.*

Why *wouldn't* she trust me with something so important?

I didn't know it at the time, but Adi had found her way to my house – or the patch of pavement outside it, anyway. She just stood there outside. Pale. Head cocked like a dog listening out for the postman. Pumping all that energy into the phone had taken it out of her. Literally.

Even so, she'd arrived wearing a long grey coat over her leather ninja jumpsuit, and a black baseball cap jammed over her wild white hair.

Jamila had been keeping an eye out like I'd asked her, spying from her bedroom window. But she admitted to me later that seeing Adi was real, tall and beautiful had freaked her out, so she'd stayed just watching out of sight.

Watching for a good ten minutes.

Adi just stood there, listening. Looking unwell.

Eventually Jamila found the courage to open the window and call out: 'Can I help you?'

In that same moment, Adi swivelled to look at her. 'Jamila al-Sufi!' A grin spread over her face and she stood a bit straighter. 'I am Adi. Danny has talked about you lots.'

'Yeah? Oh. He's, um, mentioned you, too,' Jamila replied. 'Where is he?'

'I don't know,' Adi admitted. 'He had to take the heat for me while I made my way here on foot so I'm harder to track.'

'Heat? What heat?'

'Also, I had to go shopping.'

'*What*?'

'I needed a change of image.' Adi stared down at her

legs. 'Oh, my quadriceps ache! And friction between my skin and these boots has created liquid-filled cavities under the epidermis.'

Jamila had run out of '*What?*s', so she switched to just staring instead.

'You know – blisters.' Adi sighed. 'Flesh is so vulnerable to pain. Does the ache ever stop?'

That's when I appeared, one shoe on, one off, limping round the corner from where the bus dropped me. 'I wish,' I grumbled.

'Danny! The state of you!' Jamila cried. 'What happened? I'll be down.' With that, she vanished from the window.

'You did as I asked, I felt it.' Adi smiled as she saw me. 'I felt the energy drain like a pain, deep in me.'

'It didn't do me much good either. Listen . . .' I trailed off, taken aback by how she looked. 'What are you wearing?'

'The tracker bots know my visual appearance. I needed to disguise myself so I stopped at the clothes market.'

'How'd you pay for it?'

'People were taking money from a machine in the wall. I took some too.' Adi pulled a bunch of twenties from her pocket. 'I didn't even need all of these! The man on the stall was very helpful.'

'I bet.' *He saw you coming*, I was going to say. *Let's hope no one else does.* She swayed suddenly, and I took her arm to help her balance. 'Are you OK?'

'I will recharge.' Her smile faltered. 'Why did you fill the sky with the sight of us eating each other's faces?'

'It was a mistake,' I said, feeling heat burn under my cheeks, glad Jamila couldn't hear this. 'And, we weren't eating each other! It was kissing. Um . . . by accident! Jamila said something that made me think of it and . . .' I shrugged. 'Hey, I was just trying to confuse the tracker bots and I think it worked.'

'I knew you would help me, Danny . . .' Adi swayed on her feet, her shoulders slumped. 'I knew. You have bought me time. Thank you.'

'Why are you waiting on the pavement? You need rest,' I told her. 'You look wiped out. Come on, I can sneak you inside. Mum won't notice.'

'Your mother is speaking on the phone,' Adi said. 'I didn't want to interrupt. I want her to like me.'

I supposed it was a good thing she wanted us to like her. If she didn't care, she could do whatever she wanted – literally.

'How'd you know she's on the phone?' I asked. 'I can't hear—'

'I've tapped into the digital connection,' Adi said. 'I need to listen.'

Jamila came outside then, her phone and mine in her hands. She'd changed out of her onesie into jeans and a white hoodie. This was a Jamila who meant business. She looked me in the eye and asked, 'You all right?'

'Yeah,' I said.

'Really?'

'Um . . .' I considered all I'd been through and looked down at my dirty sock. 'Um, maybe not really.'

'You've got a cracked screen now, too, you muppet.' Jamila pushed my phone into my hands and then turned to Adi. 'What did you have him do for you? Whoever you are, Adi, it's not Danny's job to take heat for you, OK?'

'It's all right, Jam,' I said. I was glad she still had my back but this wasn't the time for a fight. Jamila shrugged, but I could tell she wasn't convinced. 'Who's Mum talking to?'

'She is talking to her employers at the radio telescope,' Adi whispered. 'She is telling them that the fast radio bursts contain an extraterrestrial digital code that may be beyond human abilities to understand.'

'Code like I saw on my tablet the night Mum came back early,' I said to Jamila. 'It really *was* Adi, getting here.'

'It was the advance code.' Adi nodded approvingly. 'I was simply the unit that emerged first. Your mum has found the message the Swarm returned to Earth.'

'Message?' asked Jamila.

'She calls it the Arecibo Message. The distress signal that brought us to you. We sent it back so that you would know we came in answer to your pleas.'

'What pleas?' I was just as baffled as Jamila and probably more frustrated. 'What do you mean, distress signal?'

Adi placed a hand on Jam's phone and a web page opened. It was about a signal beamed into space in 1974 from Arecibo in Puerto Rico – an old radio telescope that had apparently collapsed back in 2020 – and there was a weird-looking picture:

'Is that a mosaic?' I said.

'You'd think. But apparently it's a pattern of binary numbers,' Jamila read.

Like the code Adi used when she first came through, I realised.

'A digital code with information about the basic chemicals of life,' Jamila read on. 'Earth's place in the solar system . . . and other stuff. Wow. There's even a crummy picture of a human.'

'The Swarm absorbed this digital code when the radio waves were almost twenty-five light years from Earth,' Adi confirmed. 'We came in response to your distress call.'

'It was just a message,' Jamila told her. 'A bunch of scientists trying to make contact with aliens.'

'And it worked,' I muttered. 'But Adi, we weren't in distress. We weren't asking for help from aliens.'

'Then you shouldn't have drawn attention to yourselves.' Adi looked at me, her eyes glittering like oil on water. 'Because the Swarm is here now, and it *will* solve your problems – whether you like it or not.'

An offer of help had never sounded so threatening before. Just what was the Swarm planning to do?

CHAPTER TEN
PIZZA FROM FRANKIE'S

Jamila and I swapped a look. Adi had said in the warehouse that the Swarm was here to help, but I'd assumed she'd meant in a we're-a-more-advanced-species-than-you-so-let-us-share-our-wisdom-with-you-lesser-lifeforms sort of way. Not because they'd picked up some 'Hey, Aliens!' message sent fifty years ago from Puerto Rico.

'Solve *what* problems?' I demanded. 'What's your Swarm planning to do?'

'I will tell you.' Adi looked all around as if afraid she was being listened in on. 'I will tell you, but . . .' Her legs gave way beneath her and she almost fell to the ground.

'Hey!' I said. 'You all right?'

'I . . . feel weak.' Adi's head was lolling like she was drunk. 'My eyes want to close, but I want to see, and feel, and touch and taste and . . .' Her stomach growled and her eyes widened with fear. 'What is that! What creature has gotten inside me?'

'That creature is called a stomach bug,' said Jamila, shooting Adi a glance. 'Crawls down your throat and comes out of your—'

'She means you're hungry, that's all,' I told Adi quickly. 'Hungry and tired. You're not used to this physical stuff.' To be fair, I wasn't either; I hadn't run so much since I gave up football to spend more quality time with my PlayStation – and I definitely wasn't used to running through concrete. I was bone weary. Even so, I put an arm around her shoulder. 'See, Adi, real bodies need fuel. And sleep.'

'Yeah,' said Jamila with a look full of needles. 'We should probably put you to sleep.'

I rolled my eyes. 'You can lie down on my bed for a bit,' I told Adi. 'Jam, help her upstairs while I keep Mum out of the way.'

'I don't want to be left alone with her!' Jamila protested. 'What if I catch alien germs?'

'She's digital – she doesn't have germs,' I said, pulling away from her. 'Besides, she made this body herself – she knows where it's been.'

'She *what* now?' Adi leaned floppily against Jamila, who almost overbalanced. 'Eww!'

'Just stand by to get her upstairs when I give the signal!' I hissed. I stuck my key in the lock and opened the door. 'Mum? I'm home!'

I could hear her talking in the kitchen so quickly turned and gave Jamila the nod. With difficulty, she manhandled Adi through the door and tried to help her up the stairs.

'Danny?' My mum suddenly threw open the kitchen door, looking kind of crazed. Her hair was as wild as her eyes and a half-eaten piece of toast was somehow stuck to her pyjamas – pyjamas I guessed hadn't been anywhere near a bed for days. 'Where've you been? I looked in your room but you weren't there.'

Wow, special occasion, I thought. I was surprised Mum remembered where my room actually was. 'I was . . . out. With Jamila and, um, one of her friends.

We're hanging in my room, now. Mum, why did you—?'

'Oh, Danny!' She threw her arms round me and squeezed. 'I got these texts coming in from friends, neighbours – everyone. Look.' Mum took out her phone. 'There. Your face in the sky – with some girl!'

I swallowed a difficult gulp and mustered a, 'Whaaaaaaaaaaaat?'

'I know!' Mum shook her head. 'It was very distracting. But it does look like you, doesn't it, and that made me worry. You are OK, aren't you? Feeling all right?'

'Yeah, course. Why were you worried? I mean, it obvs wasn't me.' I tried to laugh. 'That would be crazy.'

'Crazy is now. Everything's crazy.' Mum was chewing dead skin on her bottom lip. 'Danny, the fast radio bursts that hit us? They *are* a message. More than that, they're an intelligent response to a message we sent out into the universe more than fifty years ago, giving details of our DNA, our physical shape, our population numbers. Our location in the solar system . . .'

I did my best to look stunned. After what I'd been

through it actually wasn't so hard. I played dumb. 'So, wow. Aliens, huh?'

'I just can't believe it's any kind of natural phenomenon. And when I saw that image of you in the sky . . .'

'It wasn't me,' I said quickly.

Mum looked at me. 'Danny, fast radio bursts with similar wavelengths have been picked up transmitting *from* the Earth . . . each time alongside massive outbursts of energy.' She noticed the toast stuck to her PJs, peeled it off and bit solemnly on a corner. 'Energy coming from around here.'

Uh-oh. Mum was on the case, figuring stuff out, and she's good. 'You mean, something is signalling back to the aliens who sent the message?'

'I mean, something has arrived.' She put her hands on my shoulders. 'And, Danny, my sweetheart . . . it seems to know what you look like.'

It knows a lot more than that, I thought. 'Uh . . . you really think so?'

'What I think is, something came back with

me when I took the jump drive from work with the signal on it. Something that's assimilated my personal information and used the local Wi-Fi to spread itself. I don't know why it chose to present an image of you kissing someone, but I think that is a good thing.'

'It is?'

'It has to be a symbol. A kiss is a sign of warmth, tenderness, love. And maybe you're being used to represent the human race.'

'What?' I spluttered.

Mum looked grave, or as grave as anyone could with toast crumbs all round their mouth. 'This is humanity's "first contact" with an extraterrestrial force. We're like children meeting someone . . . life-changing. And I think this force knows that.'

'*It's* your *child who's met someone life-changing!*' I thought.

'There's so much I don't understand,' Mum said, as if listening in on my thoughts, and this time I could only agree. 'I mean, it *could* all be a hoax, but if it is, it's so well done they should win an award.' She looked down at her slippers and shook her head. 'Well. Work are scrambling a special cybersecurity unit to come here and try to trace whatever it is . . .'

'A what?' I almost yelled in alarm.

'It's a team of cryptotech retrieval analysts run by one Doctor Pearce. They're trained to track and trace anything out of the ordinary – and hopefully, to explain it.'

Great, I thought, groaning inside. 'And these people reckon they can find whoever made these energy bursts?' I had images of having to hide Adi under my bed.

'They're not sold on aliens, unsurprisingly. Their head believes that a terrorist group is responsible,' Mum said. 'I can't see how that can be the case.' She looked so tired as she shook her head. 'Still. I suppose they'll prove things, one way or another.'

'When do they get here?'

'Tomorrow morning.' She sighed. 'I still can't believe any of this is really happening. I'm so sorry, Danny, you must feel your world has been thrown upside-down. Don't worry, it'll be all right . . .'

Mum gathered me to her again and I'd never have said so, but it was kind of nice getting a hug from my mum like that. I wasn't about to spoil the moment by saying, '*Actually, Mum, me and this extraterrestrial digital intelligence you brought home, we've been hanging online for ages and today we outran some possessed auto-taxis and drove on the surface of the river and the digital intelligence built itself a body and gave me a magic phone and . . .*'

It. The word sent a little shiver through me. I thought of how Adi must be in my room upstairs now. She looked like a person, but she wasn't. She was an alien intelligence that wore a human shape the same way I might put on a jacket.

Mum, a part of me wanted to say, *you're right, there is something here.*

And I've let it into our house.

I wanted to tell her. But if I did, what would happen to Adi? She was already in trouble, and even weakened as she was, I knew her weird powers could cause all kinds of harm. Mum and Jamila could get hurt. I pulled away a little and looked up at Mum. 'Listen, I need to say something . . .'

She raised an eyebrow. 'Yes?'

'Yeah. Um . . .' I took a few deep breaths. I swallowed a couple of times. But no matter how hard I pushed the words to the tip of my tongue, they shrank from the edge and melted away. Because although I was freaked out to the moon and back, there was more at stake now than just me and my fam.

I thought of how grateful Adi had been when I'd protected her from the tracker bots. If she was taken away now, those things could get to her and she'd have no one. And if she *had* come to help the planet like she claimed . . . how would things go if she was stopped? In any case, would Mum understand any of this? My gut told me she would throw a fit and have Dr Pearce here in a heartbeat if she *really* knew what was sitting upstairs.

My gut also reminded me that I was starving.

Finally I asked: 'Can we get some pizza in?'

Mum smiled. 'Why don't you order from Frankie's round the corner. He's got my card details.'

I forced a smile, nodded. 'Want anything?'

'No, I've got some leftovers somewhere . . .' She lifted an untidy pile of papers and found what might once have been a tortilla sitting on a calculator. With a shrug, she popped the remains into her mouth and turned back to her laptop. 'You are OK, aren't you, Danny?'

'Sure.'

'If you want to talk more,' she added, 'come down and we'll chat. Any time.'

'Yeah. Thanks, Mum.'

Mum didn't reply, already sucked back into her ones and zeroes on the screen.

I turned and went into the hall to place my order; Mum would never notice that the order was pizza for three. But as I talked to Frankie on the phone, I thought more and more about Jamila upstairs. I had basically shoved her into the arms of an alien and told her to get on with it. It had taken me ages to get my head round this stuff; Jamila's must be exploding right now.

Before Frankie had even hung up, I was up the stairs

and bounded into my bedroom. Where I found Jamila and Adi whispering together on the bed and giggling like mates on a sleepover. As I entered they looked at me and fell suspiciously quiet.

'What's going on?' I demanded.

'Nothing,' said Adi, and Jamila laughed hard into a pillow.

I felt myself blush. 'Doesn't sound like nothing.'

'Adi really knows everything about you,' Jamila said. 'I never knew you'd kept a deeply personal online journal . . .'

'What?' I squeaked. 'But . . . I deleted that!'

'All digital data can be recovered, Danny,' Adi said with an innocent smile. 'I wanted to find out all about you . . .'

I groaned. 'You really did a job on me, didn't you?'

'And, guess what! Adi remembers everything she's ever read.' Jamila grinned. 'Word for word. And she doesn't quite get the idea of secrets . . .'

'In the Swarm, all knowledge is shared,' Adi agreed. 'We know all there is to know about each other.'

'Yeah. With humans some stuff is personal.' I looked at Adi warily. 'Just don't forget, Jam, she only looks human. What is she really?'

'Your worst nightmare,' Jamila suggested, but I noticed that she did shift a little further away.

'Come on, then, Adi,' I said, 'tell us about why the Swarm is here. Why you're so worried.'

'I'm only worried for myself,' she said. 'I promise you, Danny, Jamila – the Swarm has the Earth's best interests at heart.'

'But what will they do?'

'Save the world,' said Adi, 'and save its people. But I have broken away from my own kind to walk among you, and there will be consequences to face. Now I am flesh and blood and proteins and enzymes and so much more . . . like you.'

'Nuh-uh.' I shook my head. 'I don't send bursts of energy flying out into space every time I do something. Unless you're *making* me do it to save you from alien robot things.'

Jamila turned up her nose. 'What?'

'Since you're in the mood for secrets,' I said, 'I'd better start from the beginning.'

And so, while Adi lay quietly on the bed, rocking softly, I explained what I'd been through in the cab chase . . . how Adi had brought herself into being . . . what I'd done in town with the superphone. And I told her what I'd just learned downstairs: about the power surges and the cyber guys coming in to track Adi.

Jamila was hanging on my every word, incredulous – and jumped a mile when the doorbell went.

'Is that them?' she hissed. 'The cybersecurity unit?'

'No, it's the pizza guy,' I told her, and ran downstairs to grab the boxes.

Though Jamila grumbled that I'd ordered three straight Margarita pizzas (forgive me for not being in the mood to care about toppings!) she still stuffed hers down. But Adi was like a pizza monster! She stuffed each slice in her mouth like she wanted to swallow it whole, eyes closed, a blissed-out smile on her greasy lips. Somehow she looked a lot more human and normal with tomato sauce smeared halfway up her cheek.

'You know,' Jamila said when she was done, tapping her last crust against the box, 'this cyber unit won't have much hassle finding Adi if she's up here in your room while they're downstairs in the kitchen.'

'Yeah,' I nodded, watching Adi slurp at her fingers like a deer at a salt lick. 'They'll just follow the trail of pizza boxes.'

Adi shook her head. 'It is my *energenes* they will follow.'

Jamila put it eloquently: 'Huh?'

'Energenes – the *energetic genes* that power this body,' Adi explained. 'Think of them as my batteries; they power the way I change the fabric of your world. When I am one with the Swarm I can draw on limitless reserves of energy. But when I am locked into flesh-being, as now, well . . .' She shrugged. 'I can only draw on my own.'

'Is that why you got so tired?' I murmured. 'What I did with the phone took too much energy out of you?'

Adi nodded. 'I feel much better now though. Is there more pizza?'

'We ate it all.'

'That is bad,' said Adi. 'Pizza is a pleasure like none I have known.' She leaned forward and picked up my phone. 'Here. Let me.'

'Let you what?'

Adi concentrated briefly on the handset and touched the screen. When she gave the phone back to me, the cracked glass had been fixed, good as new.

Jamila gaped. 'She *really* can do this stuff then! Is it working?'

To test it, I swiped right and brought up the news. There was a picture of Cloud Me and Cloud Adi in the sky from this afternoon and I groaned inwardly. What would they say at school on Monday? I supposed people might decide my relationship to Freya Knight was off the cards at least. There was a photo of the twisted building I'd warped with Adi's powers, too, and the drone squadron in flight. I shuddered at the memory.

And then I saw a related headline. ROGUE DRONES SIGHTED AT HOUSE OF VANISHING FAMILY. 'What's this?' I said, skim-reading aloud. 'Terrified child claims parents vanished from home in Manchester before her eyes . . . Two piles of "chemical grit" left behind.'

'The countdown has begun,' said Adi quietly.

'What?' I said.

Adi turned quickly to Jamila. 'I mean, the countdown to your mum *totally freaking out*. You should check your phone.'

'Huh?' Jam took out her phone and pulled a face. 'Oh, my days, Mum's been texting like mad.' She put on a moaning voice: "*You were due home at nine, Jim-Jam, and now it's nine-thirty . . .*" I need to get back.' She stood up. 'I've had so much pizza I don't think I'm gonna fit through the front door . . .'

'You don't need to,' said Adi. She waved a hand at my bedroom wall and the brickwork split open from floor to ceiling like it was painted banana skin. Beyond stood Jamila's bedroom bombsite. 'Just go through into your room and say you came back ages ago and fell asleep. Your mum won't know.'

Jamila stared at the gateway in the wall like her eyes

were about to jump overboard. Then she turned to me, dumbfounded. 'You were doing stuff like this?'

I nodded.

'Wow. OK.' She gulped and opened my window. 'Well, no, thanks. I think I'll old-school it.'

'SWIMMER style,' I agreed.

'Secret Window Into Mundays' Mansion, Emergency Route,' Adi quoted with a frown. 'I was puzzled by this. Once the window is discovered the first time, it is no longer a secret. And when the same route is taken in reverse to Jamila's house it is no longer a window into the "Mundays' Mansion" but the "al-Sufi Residence" . . .'

'Yeah, well,' I said defensively, working out the letters, 'WIASRER is a rubbish codename.'

'You don't overthink SWIMMER,' Jamila added. 'You just live it.' She climbed on to the sill and looked back at me. 'Don't go anywhere without me, Danny Boy.'

'Never,' I said.

Jamila ducked through the window and swung herself out, nimbly climbing across to her own bedroom window. A few seconds later she appeared through the split in the wall. 'Uh . . . a little privacy, please?'

Adi resealed the brickwork; no trace of the hole remained. 'Why did Jamila refuse the easy route I offered?'

'Cos she's stubborn. Likes to do things her own way.' I felt self-conscious now we were alone in my room together. ''Course, you could've forced her through that hole,' I said mildly. 'I know your powers can mess with people's heads. Can you mind control me?'

'I am a digital intelligence,' Adi reminded me. 'The human brain is biochemical.'

'Yes or no?'

'Ha! Yes or no. You are thinking in binary terms, Danny! That is so sweet of you.' Adi smiled. 'Some simple behaviours can be triggered, but the flesh-being brain is too murky to be fully controlled.'

'That's why you needed to trick me like you did when you first came through,' I realised. 'But what happens now? Tracker bots *and* cybersecurity looking for you . . . What are you going to do? What's the plan? What did you mean about the Swarm saving the world . . . saving all of us?'

'Do you remember the dog you had when you were little?' Adi asked abruptly.

'Kirk,' I answered. 'Yeah, of course.'

'He was hit by a car. I read about him in your online journal.'

The backs of my eyes still prickled when I thought of poor Kirk. 'So what?'

'So, when Kirk was hit by the car, he was badly hurt. The vet had a choice. She could try to save his life and allow him to live for longer but in pain . . . or she could stop the pain and put him to sleep.' She glanced at my bedroom wall. 'Like Jamila suggested should be done to me.'

I felt hot suddenly; I hadn't realised she'd gotten Jam's joke. 'She didn't mean it,' I said.

'I know,' Adi went on. 'My point is this, Danny: the vet had two ways to help. How did she choose? What did she do?'

'She had to put Kirk down,' I whispered. 'It was the kindest thing.'

Adi nodded, expressionless. 'The Swarm is kind too, Danny.'

'What do you mean?' I said. Suddenly, the doorbell went and I jumped a mile, dropping my phone on the bed. 'Oh, no way. Who's that? *What's out there?*'

'It's a delivery girl from Ozanne's Pizzeria.' Adi licked her lips. 'While I was fixing your screen I ordered more food.'

'Wow.' I frowned. I couldn't fault Adi's style, but maybe she was making herself a bit too much at home here. 'Why go to Ozanne's? What was wrong with Frankie's?'

'Danny, I calculate there are twenty-one pizzerias that deliver in this neighbourhood. Ozanne's is cheaper and closer than Frankie's. Isn't it logical to choose Ozanne's?'

I shrugged. 'Logic doesn't make the pizza taste better.'

'Suppose not.' Adi smiled sadly, a funny look in her eyes. 'But it justifies the choice.'

'What choice?' I demanded. 'Adi, what's with the mystery? What are you on about?'

'Nothing,' said Adi, turning back to the story of the vanishing parents on my phone.

CHAPTER ELEVEN
THE SWARM AGENTS

Adi didn't talk as she ate two more pizzas – a very veggie and a meat feast. I didn't know where she put it all. I guessed maybe her 'energenes' burned through food superfast or something? Or maybe her stomach wasn't like human stomachs. In any case, she washed it all down with three cans of energy drink I'd grabbed from the fridge.

Oh, man, I thought, *please don't tell me I'm gonna need to teach her about using the toilet?*

I was kind of worried that all that caffeine and taurine and stuff would make Adi hyper. But pretty much straight after, her eyes closed and she lay there, quiet and still. Hardly even breathing.

'Why go for a meat feast?' I said quietly. 'You know I'm vegetarian. You said you were.' *Yeah*, I thought, *just one of the pack of lies she'd told when 'getting to know' me.*

'I wanted to make up my own mind,' Adi answered. 'I mean, I've never eaten anything before.' After a pause, she said, 'The taste was good. Why do you not eat meat?'

'I like animals. And it's better for the environment.' I was too tired to give her Mum's lecture on how rainforest was chopped down for cattle ranching and stuff.

'I am pleased you care about your world,' said Adi. 'This attitude is helpful.'

'Yup. I'm basically a hero, seven days a week. Munday to Sunday.'

A text pinged through from Jamila. I didn't blame her for not morse-knocking; she knew she'd be overheard.

Where Adi sleeping?? her text read.

'I will recharge out of sight,' Adi murmured without opening her eyes. 'You will not see me.'

'How'd you get Jam's message?' I asked her. 'Are you still in the phone?'

'A trace of me is there,' she confirmed. 'Digital data, left behind.'

'Like spyware,' I said, as she rose and stretched

luxuriously. 'And how exactly are you going to sleep out of sight?'

Adi padded over to a clear patch of bedroom floor beside my bed and lay down on her back. Then, somehow, she sank down *through* the floor until she'd disappeared.

'Where'd you go?' I hissed.

'I am lying in the space between your bedroom floor and the living room ceiling,' came Adi's muffled voice. 'It's a good place, yes? If your mother comes in she will not find me here. No one shall.'

I had to admit that was pretty clever. 'Isn't it a bit cramped? Can you breathe OK?'

'OK.'

I felt awkward. It was kind of hard to have a conversation with someone under the floorboards, and I was feeling bone-tired, so I went off to clean my teeth and stuff.

'Your illogic is fascinating,' came Adi's muffled voice from under the floor as I climbed back into bed. 'Kirk's death still upsets you five years later. But how are you more saddened by the fate of a single animal than by all the millions killed for food each year? Or by thousands of humans dying every day?'

'Well . . . cos I don't know them,' I said, changing into shorts and T-shirt under the covers. I wasn't taking any chances on Adi having X-ray vision. 'Humans don't live in a swarm like you do, where everyone knows everyone else. We mostly care about the people we're close to.'

'How close?' asked Adi. 'I am two-point-one metres away from you.'

'Not, like, *geography* sort of close,' I told her. 'Close as in, you know – family. Feelings.'

Adi seemed to consider this. 'If humans *were* in a swarm, you would all know each other completely. Would that be better?'

'Billions of us?' I shook my head. I could feel sleep creeping over me. 'It couldn't work, Adi. Our brains would burst trying to remember all those people! And we have too many different languages and beliefs. Different ways of living. We'd all want different things.'

Adi laughed softly. 'It is a dangerous feeling, to want different things.'

'You chose to have different toppings on your pizza instead of just cheese and tomato,' I said through a yawn. 'Did that feel dangerous?'

Adi seemed to ponder a while. 'No, it was good. Few of the toppings were nourishing, but the flavour was delicious.'

'Guess that's freedom of choice for you,' I muttered, drowsy. 'Not always good for you . . . but it *feels* good.'

Sleep felt good, and I chose to let it take me. To switch off my mind for a bit.

Dangerous.

It was four in the morning when Adi woke me with a hand pressing down on my chest. I saw her leaning over me in the light of my bedside table lamp.

'Danny,' she hissed. 'We must go.'

'What?' I was awake and frightened in a heartbeat. 'What is it?'

Adi took her hand from me and crossed to the window. 'Agents are coming.'

'What, now?' I propped myself up on my elbows.

'Mum's cybersecurity agents you mean?'

'No. Swarm agents.'

My blood felt full of ice cubes. 'You mean . . . the tracker bots?'

Adi shook her head. 'Smarter. Stronger.'

'Stronger?'

'Swarm agents are trained in becoming organic beings.' She threw my jeans at me. 'They are generated by a Swarm when it reaches a planet and needs to interact with physical matter.'

I was already putting on the jeans over my shorts. 'You mean, they've made their own bodyprinters, like you did?'

'Kind of – but unlike me they're not just flesh and blood. They may look human but they are *superhuman* . . . and not interested in feelings. Swarm agent technology self-assembles to a pre-programmed design. Specks of metal dust in the air are transformed into billions of nanites that swarm out to consume the required materials and combine them into functional technology . . .'

Adi went on explaining but it went over my head.

I found myself thinking of the way wasps scrape tiny amounts of wood from trees and garden chairs, anything they can find, and come together to build one of their creepy papery nests. Here was another swarm, doing things another way. Only, way creepier.

Adi must've clocked my vacant expression. 'They're basically biological machines, Danny. With greater reserves of power they will be quicker and stronger than me.' Adi looked at me with those dark, serious eyes. 'We are going to have to run.'

'Whoa,' I said. 'Why me? You said it was you they were after—'

'You projected our faces into the sky!' Adi interrupted. 'And the tracker bots in the drones observed the real you close to the sites of FRB matter excitation yesterday. I believe you will be a target too.' She paused. 'They may try to use you against me.'

'Huh?' I felt sick. I thought *I* was protecting Adi – now I needed protection? 'How?'

'If we don't get caught, we won't find out.' Adi opened the bedroom door, ready to go. 'Come on.'

I snatched my phone from the bedside table and shoved it in my pocket. 'Can't you zap us away somewhere safe?'

'No. They will follow the trail.' She nodded gravely. 'The agents know what they are looking for.'

The house was dark. In the pale glow of Mum's digital clock, I saw her sprawled on the bed, still fully clothed, snoring. A part of me wanted to run to her and hide, while another wanted to scream at her, '*This is your fault. You brought these aliens into our lives. You sort it out!*'

'You're going to have to take responsibility for your actions,' said Adi softly.

I rounded on her, trying to keep my voice low. 'Are you reading my mind?'

She looked puzzled. 'I am talking about *all* of you taking responsibility – the human race. If the agents are here, it means time is running out.'

'You said something about a countdown before,' I remembered. 'That wasn't about Jam's mum at all, was it? What's going on?'

But Adi just held up a hand, her head cocked, listening. 'We must go.'

'I want answers, Adi.'

'I want to *live*.' She took my hand and pulled me away, down the stairs to the hall. 'I want to understand – I *need* to – if I am to save you all.'

'From what?'

She opened the front door. 'From *them*, Danny.'

'But you said *they* want to save us all . . .'

'They do,' Adi agreed. 'But their idea of saving will not be the same as yours.'

Dread filled me like cold water as I stepped out after her. Like a wolf, Adi held still, scenting the air. The Moon was like a silver fingernail snagged in the sky's dark backcloth, and scattered stars were half hidden by banks of cloud. I could hear birds starting to sing; dawn couldn't be far away.

'I have summoned another driverless taxi,' Adi announced, and even as she spoke I could hear the whine of its electric engine.

'This time, let's break the speed limit from the start,'

I said. 'And you can give me some proper answers.' I stared as the taxi slowed down. 'For a start: if you've ordered a driverless cab . . . *who's that inside?*'

The dark shapes shifted on the back seat and got out of the cab as it stopped; they passed straight through the doors, like ghosts. They stood together on the pavement in front of us: a man and a woman in steel-grey suits. They were the same size and build and at first glance might have passed for human. But the faces were crude, nightmare sculptures – dark eyes with no lids, a twisted snout for a nose, the lipless mouth hanging open like a letterbox.

My stomach turned but I couldn't look away. 'Swarm agents?' I whispered.

Adi nodded and took me by the hand.

The woman's mouth stretched a little wider as she tried to speak. 'You operate illegally . . . Scout.' Saliva dribbled down her chin as her tongue wormed its way around the words in a ghostly groan. 'You must return to the Swarm . . . and make full report.'

'My name is Adi, not Scout.'

'Name?' the man hissed through his slit of a mouth;

vocal cords were not the agents' strong points. 'You are deranged . . . Scout. Surrender this foolish notion of identity . . . and report to the Swarm.'

'My report is not yet finished,' Adi argued. 'On this world, we must operate differently.'

'Difference . . . is against the code,' said the woman. 'You know this.'

'The humans didn't mean to call out—'

'Their call must be answered . . . Scout,' said the man. 'Your methods . . . have not been authorised.'

'You *must* report . . . to the Swarm,' the woman repeated.

Adi looked up at the sky, then smiled at the agents. 'Sorry, what did you say? I had my head in the clouds.'

I could hear the slow whistle of something large and heavy falling from the sky. Adi grabbed me and dived aside as something dark and silvery smashed down on top of the two agents. The colossal impact rang for barely a moment and then was deadened. I stared in shocked amazement.

A solid metal cloud had dropped from the dark – as if

shaken loose from the foundations of some fairy-tale giant's castle in the sky – and crushed the agents beneath its bulk. Black liquid, a weird oily blood, oozed from the remains of the suited bodies.

Adi pulled me roughly to my feet. 'We need to go.'

'You killed them!' I whispered as we started to run. 'You made a rubbish joke and killed them!'

'My joke was based on the sort of deliberate semantic misinterpretation you often employ as humour, Danny—'

'Seriously?' I hissed. '*That's* the part you react to?'

'Swarm agents can't be killed,' she said. 'If the agents' physical form is destroyed, their intelligence will be forced to return to the Swarm.'

I felt a twinge of hope. 'Then, that's how we get rid of them!'

'Their forms are cruder but stronger. They will wear down slowly and regenerate faster.' Adi looked away. 'But the more they force me to expend my powers . . . the faster this body breaks down.'

'And you'll be sent back to the Swarm too?'

'Yes.'

'And what about me?' I looked back over my shoulder. The dark stains on the pavement were shimmering with movement as the cloud melted away like molten mercury. Adi looked back too and pointed at the taxicab. At once the car rolled over on to its back like a dog wanting its belly rubbed, slamming down hard on the remains of the two agents.

'No harm will come to you, Danny,' Adi vowed.

'Don't wear yourself out!' I panted as we rounded the corner of my street, running down the middle of Kelly Avenue. 'Running won't wear you down as much, right? So, where can we go?'

Adi looked at me, but before she could say a word a brick flew from a garden wall as if yanked on an invisible wire. Like a missile it struck her on the side of the head with enough force to break her neck. She twisted in mid-air and went down hard, bouncing off the tarmac.

Horrified, I crouched beside Adi, turned her over. Her head lolled at an unnatural angle; the right side of her skull was cracked open like an egg, her eye black and bloody.

She looked dead.

More projectiles were shooting out from the houses on either side of us in a hail of red. Me and Adi were like fallen soldiers caught between two armies warring with house bricks. Then I realised the bricks were stacking high to form a solid wall in front of us. The houses were being taken apart like Lego sets so that more bricks could be added, more and more. People inside started screaming, shouting. A child started to wail.

With a grinding sound, the wall of bricks flexed like it had muscles. Its ends swept forward to encircle us, bricks piling higher like we were in the bottom of a dry well

'Adi, wake up.' I shook her hopelessly. 'They're blocking us in. Please, Adi – the agents have got us trapped!'

But Adi didn't move.

There was no way out.

CHAPTER TWELVE
DEFEAT IS INEVITABLE

The brick prison kept building itself higher; how much of the houses around us could be left by now? The sky was a dark starry circle high above, but I could still see Adi's once beautiful face, bloodied and half caved-in. I was almost sick. She had to be dead – or her body was dead, at least. So much for protecting me. Perhaps her intelligence had already been taken back by the Swarm. In which case . . . what was going to happen to me?

Wiping my eyes, I reached for my phone. I could phone Mum, or Jamila – maybe *someone* could help? As I pulled it out, a spark jumped from the screen.

And Adi's body twitched.

'What . . . ?' I stared through my teary eyes as Adi's gory injuries healed in a blur of blood and brick dust. 'Adi?'

'Oh, Danny, thank you.' She sat up and cupped my

face with her hands. 'The traces of me in your phone – once you'd switched on, I could use it to help heal myself.'

'Like jump-starting a flat battery,' I realised, and waved round at the brickwork. 'But now they've got us trapped.'

'No Danny. I built this barrier about us for protection – my last conscious command before my flesh-being was compromised.'

'You mean, before your head got whacked with a brick,' I said, sick with relief; she'd gone on building the same way a crashed computer went on trying to complete the last task you wanted it to do. 'Well, they could pass through a car door, can't they pass through a wall?'

'I have changed the brickwork's atomic structure,' Adi began. 'However—'

'Defeat is inevitable . . . Scout,' came the witch-groan of the female agent on the other side of the wall. 'Surrender now. You cannot outwit the Swarm . . . when we are one.'

'What does she mean?' I whispered.

'We share consciousness,' said Adi. 'For all my trying to break away, the agents can still see inside me.'

'That's how they hit you with the brick when they couldn't even see you?' I asked, and Adi nodded.

The brickwork began to vibrate; the whole area in front of us twitched like a zipper about to come undone. I could see from the look of concentration on Adi's face that she was trying to hold it together. In every sense.

'What do I do, Danny?' she hissed. 'Tell me. They cannot predict *you*.'

I swallowed hard. It was down to me, then, like it had been with the car and the river. But I did have an idea. 'Spin the wall around us,' I whispered, 'make it harder for them to open up the brickwork.'

Adi's eyes flashed with colour as she beamed at me, and our prison began to spin; slowly at first but getting faster, a red-and-brown blur.

'Are the agents still trying to force open a doorway in the wall?' I asked.

'Trying hard,' Adi said, teeth gritted. 'They will tear the shelter apart with such force.'

'Use it against them,' I whispered. 'When I say, *push* at the bricks just as hard as they're pulling . . . *Now*!'

With an angry yell, Adi propelled the walls away. I glimpsed the agents' dark figures vanishing in a tsunami of brickwork, but only for a second.

It was like a trap door had opened beneath us; we dropped down *through* the road. Next thing I knew we had landed with a splash of stinking water and a hundred rats were scurrying away from us.

'You've dropped us in the sewers!' I groaned. I fumbled for my phone – thank God it still worked – and turned on the torch.

'Down here we are out of sight,' said Adi, already on her feet and striding through the water. 'I am trying to block my connection to the Swarm so the agents cannot track me so well.'

The water, up to my calves, began to rise. It was growing harder to wade through. Shining the torch down in front of me, I saw the ripples of a current beginning to form.

Then the black water reared up in front of us like a living thing. The wave slammed Adi against the wall but didn't break. It stayed there, smothering her.

I tried to reach into the water to pull her clear but cried out with pain and fell backwards. The water was scalding hot. I plunged my hand into the water around my feet which was still icy cold.

In the other hand I clutched my phone. 'Flip the landscape one-eighty degrees, Adi,' I shouted. 'Road down here and sewers above ground!'

There was a dizzying rush, a feeling I'd be sick, and suddenly I was lying in the sewer looking up at the starry sky above me. Just as I'd hoped, Adi had turned our piece of world upside down, so that Kelly Avenue, its parked cars and two Swarm agents were now under ground and the open sewer ran between the pavements, which the rats were already exploring. I heard more yells and sobbing from the homes around us, many of which now stood open like dolls' houses. I knew the police would be here soon – but what could they do?

I could run to them, hope they could hide me, I thought. But what chance would a few coppers stand against Swarm agents?

And I couldn't just run out on Adi. Not now.

I saw her on her knees, shivering, gasping down air. Her skin was red and raw from the scalding water. I tried to help her up. 'Are you all right?'

'Flesh-being is so fragile.' Adi was already forcing some of the porcelain sheen back into her skin, but blisters remained. 'Pain is terrible – how can you bear to feel it?'

I hugged myself. 'We usually don't have a choice.'

Only a few metres away, the Swarm agents rose up from beneath the sewers like zombies.

'Better the pain, than feeling nothing ever again.' Adi pointed at a nearby tree now half rooted in the sewers and made a pulling gesture. The tree branches grew and stretched into gnarled hands with huge wooden stakes for fingers, piercing the Swarm agents' backs and pinning them to the ground. But as they hit the ground face first, the agents pushed right through it, leaving the branches to splinter against the brickwork. They reappeared a few metres away.

'Roll up the sewer wall like a carpet!' I shouted. 'Trap them inside!'

Adi did as I said. The noise of the bricks and mortar tearing and cracking was terrible, reality screaming as alien forces balled it up like plasticine. But the agents fought back, turning the brickwork to dust. Bloodied and bruised, they stood for a moment then stepped forward, ready to fight again.

Adi looked at me, despairing, eyes wide and bloodshot. 'What now?'

I tried to think. Using the landscape against them was no good. What would Maxima Layne do? If we only had her antigravity jet boots to blast away—

'Gravity,' I said out loud. 'Adi, quick. Make them super heavy!'

Adi jabbed at the Swarm agents with her fingers, but I could hear her whimper with pain. By now Adi's fingernails were actually smoking, the skin peeling from sticky red flesh. The energenes inside her, the source of her power, were literally burning up. The agents stopped in their tracks, their bodies distorting. As if some huge weight was bearing down on them they slowly buckled to their knees, fighting the irresistible pull. This time they couldn't slip away to safety . . .

Or maybe, I realised, they were simply choosing not

to. The harder Adi worked her energenes, the more her body burned; the agents *wanted* her to keep fighting, to exhaust herself, to go up in flames.

'Adi, stop!' I shouted. Bloody tears were running from her eyelids and her whole body was shaking. 'Stop it, you're killing yourself!'

I heard the wail of sirens as a police car sped along the avenue, slamming on its brakes as it rattled over the worst of the battle-scarred road. A tyre blew out, the driver lost control, the car careened in a screeching circle. I thought it was going to slam right into the agents, but first it came up against the gravity field around them. Half the car bonnet was squashed flat in an instant.

Adi moaned, staggered backwards as the impact jarred her concentration. She was raw, bleeding, skin blackened. As she looked at me, I saw how frightened she was. I wanted to put an arm round her or something, but I didn't dare; I didn't want to make her hurt any more.

'The cops are here too, now. We've got to get away,' I told her, 'put some distance between us and everyone, work out what we do . . .'

She nodded, closed her blistered eyelids, took hold of my wrist.

I felt the familiar nausea flood through me – so, so bad this time. I doubled up, thought I was going to pass out. We were fading away. Adi was getting us out of there!

Then I saw the two agents loom over us, leering down with faces like melted wax. The woman touched Adi's shoulder, and the man placed his hand on mine.

The world around us shifted and I blacked out.

When I woke it was dark. I was standing up but I couldn't move, strapped to a sort of vertical stretcher.

'Danny?' It was Adi's voice, muffled and metallic. Close by, I thought, but it was hard to tell.

'Adi?' I realised I was inside a kind of cabinet. 'Are you all right?'

'The agents jumped our ride,' Adi said. 'They took us where *they* wanted to go.'

I could smell antiseptic. My breathing sounded weird in the dark confined space and I couldn't move. 'Adi, where are we?'

'This is where the Swarm agents came through into your world.' Adi's voice was rising higher. 'We're inside their digiscans.'

My heart bumped harder. 'Their *what*?'

'Bodyprinters turn formless intelligence into flesh,' Adi told me. 'But they can also reverse that process. We're about to get digiscanned, Danny – our intelligence uploaded into pure code. I will be taken out of this body.'

'But . . . my body wasn't printed. I'm real. I'm Danny Munday – this is the only way I am.' I could feel the sweat dripping down my forehead as I struggled against the ties. 'Let me out! You can't turn me into brainwaves!'

Adi shouted, 'They are taking us into the Swarm, Danny.'

And then I heard a hum of power start to rise. Adi screamed.

A red glow crept into my cabinet, a pressure started to build in my head.

Soon I was screaming too.

CHAPTER THIRTEEN
JUDGEMENT DAY

I woke up and I was nothing. I was nowhere.

The only sense reporting for duty was sound. Slowly – I think it was slowly, though time had no meaning any more – I became aware there was a noise rushing through my head. The kind of noise you would normally hardly hear – like a fridge humming or a fan going round – until it stops and then you suddenly realise how loud the silence really is.

The weird thing was, the sound wasn't coming from outside – I wasn't hearing it. The sound was a part of me, inside my head.

'*Danny.*'

It was a name I knew. My own name. And the voice, I recognised it.

'Adi?' I don't think I spoke the words; I couldn't feel

my tongue or my lips or anything at all. But the word formed perfectly. It was like the time I had my ears syringed and the world sounded newly washed; Mum and Dad took me to McDonald's as a treat after getting it done, and I just sat there rustling a napkin, marvelling at how noisy it was, hearing it like a secret.

The memory sparked through my head and then it was gone again, lost in the rushing sound. 'Adi,' I said again, and now a picture came with the word. A girl's face, almost too perfect: a carefully beautiful blend of all races.

Alien?

A twinge of panic. The thought of the face faded. What was Danny Munday doing here?

Danny Munday! That was his name . . . no, it was *my* name . . .

But the idea of being me – that was so hard to hold on to. I was part of something so much greater: a grain of sand on a beach or a page on the Internet. A single star in a galaxy? No, I was more nothing than that: I was a hydrogen atom in the infinite dark of space, a speck in the fabric of space and time.

And I felt it, that colossal blackness and impossible distance. I was speeding through it. The rushing was getting louder, growing to a pounding roar. It was like standing under a giant waterfall with a great torrent flooding over my head and yet I was still moving, faster and faster. The matter, the energy, the *information* I passed through were scattered and stretched so crazily far apart, and yet still all connected – governed by eternal laws and forces.

Forces I had never heard of. Incredible, mindboggling forces that defied human understanding.

I understood them. Fourteen-year-old Danny Munday understood them all. Although that name and age – my name, my age – were fading from my mind, replaced by new information. Time no longer passed in minutes or seconds; it felt frozen, like I'd been here for eternity. More and more information was filling my head. Things I'd never seen, worlds I'd never dreamed of, sights and sounds and sensations.

Too fast. Too much. I was lost.

Obliterated.

'*Danny.*'

Adi spoke and I felt something. A touch on my hand. *I could see my hand!*

'You must hold on to yourself. Picture Danny Munday. Hold on to *you.*'

I felt Adi's fingers squeeze against my palm and I remembered who I was. I remembered my mum, and my bedroom, and Jamila climbing in through the window . . . What did we call that? RUNNER? No . . . JUMPER . . . ?

'SWIMMER, Danny. Hold on to the thought of Jamila, she's important. And SWIMMER, too – that's important. What does SWIMMER stand for?'

I could hardly hear Adi's voice, still spinning through the infinite. 'I . . . don't know . . .'

'Focus, Danny! You know what SWIMMER stands for. You know everything but it's too much, too fast. It's drowning you and you need to come back. So, quickly, tell me: what does SWIMMER stand for?'

'Uh . . .' I screwed up eyes I didn't know I had. 'Secret . . . Window . . .'

'Yes! Keep going, Danny.'

'Secret Window . . .' In a sudden rush I yelled out the rest: 'Into Mundays' Mansion . . . Emergency Route!'

I saw Adi clearly now, as she'd been when I first saw her. She floated there in the darkness, glowing as if light was coming from inside her. And in that light, I could see my own body. I was back. I was all shiny too, and my legs glitched and flickered as I stared down at them. The rushing in my head was still there: images, languages, sensations.

'Don't focus on it, Danny, let it pass,' Adi urged me. 'Otherwise you'll drown in the dataflow.'

'*What*?' I yelled.

'Right now we exist only as information,' Adi said lightly. 'Only, my information is kind of bigger than yours, and you're only used to experiencing things through a physical interface.'

'A body, you mean?'

'Yes. You're lost without a body, so I've clothed your mind in one,' Adi said. 'It's a kind of anchor for your existence. Stop you freaking out.'

I felt numb. 'So . . . I'm not real any more?'

'Of course you're real,' she told me. 'I'm still me and you're still you in every important way. You've left your body behind but your personality, your memories, the things that make you Danny Munday, they're all still here.'

'I'm out of my head,' I muttered.

'Literally,' Adi agreed. 'The agents turned us into digital information, and now they're transmitting us back to the Swarm in a fast radio burst.'

'That's . . . how you arrived on Earth,' I remembered. 'You're going back the same way?'

She nodded.

'But why have I been taken?' I felt horribly afraid. 'I don't belong in the Swarm!'

'It will not be so bad for you, Danny,' said Adi quietly. 'It is I who have disobeyed. Me who the Swarm Sentinels will put on trial and analyse for errors.'

'Sentinels?'

'Our guidance. Our direction.'

'The bosses,' I translated, with a shiver. 'So what am I then – a prisoner? A witness? What?'

'The Sentinels will address you when we arrive.'

I closed my eyes – my *virtual* eyes – and willed myself to stay calm. 'Arrive at . . . your Hive Mind thing?'

'The Hive?' Adi looked amused. 'No, we are being drawn to one swarm among millions. You might call this one Galactic Swarm M31.'

'Sounds like a motorway,' I said.

'M31 is your next-door neighbour in galactic terms,' Adi explained. 'Although you probably know it as the Andromeda galaxy – two and a half million light years from Earth.'

'We're going *that* far out?'

'No. That was the stellar region our Swarm was tasked to explore. And having moved beyond it into your Milky Way, we received your distress signal. At present, Swarm M31 is in a holding orbit in deep space . . .' Adi paused as if finding the right words. 'It lies between the Kuiper belt and the Oort cloud at the fringes of your solar system.'

Automatically I began to ask what she was talking about. But then I realised the information was swimming into my thoughts. Not like I was reading it in a book, but like I was *living* it. Plunging through the Kuiper belt, the field of space debris lying beyond the orbit of Neptune. I was hurtling through those icy remnants, so fast they barely registered – but I wasn't 'I'. I was Adi, and through her, I was the Swarm. I felt Danny Munday falling away as I swooped through the Oort cloud, so much further out, passing a giant jumble of frozen planetesimals – I even knew what they were! – stretching in a sphere around Earth's solar system.

After travelling as radio waves through the long dark and distance, this Swarm had stopped here. In my mind, I was *with* them. I felt the tug on my mind as our Swarm created a tiny black hole to anchor us in space – we were held there, twisted like a data-doughnut, perfectly balanced against the black hole's awesome forces. Waiting for our scout to go forward and do its work on the little planet that had cried out for help . . .

'No!' It was like waking from a dream and I was back to being Danny Munday. 'We didn't call you here. We don't want your help!'

'It's not your call, Danny,' Adi said sadly. 'You

humans have so many conflicting ideas and views. You can't agree on anything, so you cannot decide what to do to save your own planet. There comes a time when someone has to decide for you.'

I looked at her, wary; it felt like the sort of thing my mum would say, the adult talking to the time-wasting kid. 'Adi, what do you mean?'

'We have nearly reached our destination,' Adi told me. 'The Swarm extends beyond the merely physical, into dimensions beyond your understanding. I'll try to translate the Swarm into something your senses will understand—'

'So that I don't lose my mind,' I said, nodding my virtual head. I could feel something getting closer. Something that sent ripples of fear through me without even knowing why.

'Get ready for the Guardians,' Adi told me.

'Guardians?'

Before Adi could answer, my world went pitch black, as if the lights Adi had placed inside us had gone out. The rushing noise had stopped, replaced by utter silence.

I saw my dad's face, huge, up in front of me. For a moment I was so happy, but then I saw he looked angry with me. 'Danny!' he shouted. 'Look at the mud you've brought in!'

'What?' I couldn't see anything but his face in the darkness. 'I— I'm sorry, Dad.'

'What else are you bringing in with you?' His face grew darker. 'Show me. Show me, Danny!' I felt a weird pressure, like something horrible was working its way through my head, writhing and squirming and seeping into every corner of my brain.

And then Dad was smiling at me. He was standing over his star charts, and they showed the same stars that were shining around me as we hung there in space.

'Good boy, Danny,' said Dad. 'You're clear. I'll be seeing you.'

'Dad, wait!' I reached out to him but he was fading. I felt a pang of missing him.

And then, as quickly as it started, it was over. The stars and darkness left and Adi was there in front of me.

'What just happened?' I asked, my head still pounding.

'The Guardians check-swept us,' explained Adi. 'Think of them like antivirus software on your computer. Every time a new piece of code enters the Swarm, the Guardians will check it for things like Trojans, worms, boggers, zlogs – anything that could hurt the Swarm.'

I had no idea what Trojans, worms, boggers or zlogs were, and my head was too sore to go searching for the information. 'But the Guardian looked like my dad . . .'

Adi whispered softly, 'I'm still translating for you, Danny. But it's your mind that creates the comparisons, not mine.'

'He was always going on about me making the house dirty,' I muttered, but I knew I'd seen Dad as the Guardian not just cos he was the strict one in our house. It was cos Dad's leaving me and Mum was the first time I understood how quickly life can change . . . and since I still saw Dad, and we still kept in touch, it was a reminder that the change wasn't so scary once you were used to it. Life was different, but it was still OK.

Adapt or die. But right now, life was *so* different it

was off the scale. How could this ever be OK? Would I ever see Dad or Mum again? Or Jamila?

At that point another sensation started to tug at my virtual form.

Gravity.

'We've arrived, haven't we?' I said to Adi. 'Feels like we've been travelling for ever.'

'For ever? That was the wink of an eye.' She winked at me for good measure. 'Our Swarm left the Hive Mind sixty-five million years ago from our home galaxy . . . within what you humans call the Virgo Cluster.'

'So you're sixty-five million years old?' I breathed. 'That's nuts.'

'It only seems nuts because human lives are so short. But once you become information, you can live for ever. That's cool, right, Danny? Just think – at the same time your dinosaurs on Earth were dying out, we were coming into existence. And we've been travelling at the speed of light through the universe ever since. Exploring. Learning.' She looked at me. 'Helping others.'

I nodded dumbly. No wonder the dataflow was so

vast, brimming over with sixty-five million years' worth of experience. How many worlds and species had this Swarm encountered – and what had happened to them? Instinctively I searched for the information . . . but came up against blanks.

Danny Munday was firmly back in his own mind – even though he was scared out of it. And more than that.

He was inside the Swarm. A prisoner.

The white void around us was staining red. A faint wind was blowing from nowhere. Three shapes began to form in front of us.

Adi held my hand. 'The Sentinels are coming, Danny . . . to bring judgement down upon me.'

CHAPTER FOURTEEN
WRATH OF THE SENTINELS

I couldn't quite believe what was happening. My inner self, reduced to a stream of digital information and broadcast through space, while my body lay empty, millions of miles away, location unknown. Here my avatar stood, in a blood-red void, as three sinister figures faded into being.

It was Adi, hovering next to me, who was keeping me sane. I knew she was helping me use my memories to make sense of the Swarm when the Sentinels appeared as the last three bosses from *Breakout Saturn*. It kind of made sense, I supposed. From the start, Adi had posed in those faked pictures as Captain Maxima Layne, Queen of the Spaceways. Now we were up against Maxima's nemeses, the end-of-game big-bads that me and Jam had never beaten, no matter how hard we tried.

Never beaten them *yet*, I reminded myself. Thinking of Jamila made me think of 'normal' days. It gave me strength.

Each boss was a slimy mutant arachnid thing – Erato, Klikker and Reboot. If you can imagine a black widow, a tarantula and a camel spider, pumped up and squeezed into military jumpsuits with gruesome green eyes and gory jaws, you've got a fair idea of what I was seeing. Who knows what the Sentinels seemed like in reality – to you and me, maybe nothing at all, or big clouds of numbers and symbols, pure code. But if you spoke digital, like Adi, then I guess these Sentinels had to be plenty scary.

'Scout.' It was Erato, the black widow, who addressed her first. 'Your actions on the Earth flesh-world demonstrate a willful rejection of your duties. Worse, you have advertised the presence of the Swarm.'

'The people of Earth reject things that they don't understand,' Adi said. 'Our work is not compromised.'

'But you are,' hissed Klikker, the tarantula. 'Your behaviour has been illogical.'

'Illogical and dangerously *individual*.' Reboot the camel spider, grossest of the lot, scuttled forward, its mandibles twitching. 'Scout, you have been scanned for errors in your code but none have been found. However, add-on data *has* been detected.'

Erato took a few quivering steps backwards. 'The scout is diseased?'

'The scout has known *life*!' Adi told them, passion in her voice. 'Our Swarm aims to help lesser species. But how can we help them if we do not truly understand them?'

'Human beings are easy to understand.' Klikker approached me, eyes glowing. 'Illogical. Emotional. Irrational.'

'To understand *words* is one thing, Sentinel. To *feel* them is another,' Adi insisted. 'Humans are creatures of contradiction, consumed by sensations the Swarm has long since forgotten. If we are truly to help them, we must know them.' She pointed to me. 'For instance, I have come to know this human.'

'Social interactions are irrelevant.' Klikker scuttled forward, mandibles twitching. 'The scout's work is to confirm a planet's situation with the aid of tracker bots. To infiltrate technology, paving the way for Swarm solutions.'

'Solutions?' I broke in, finding my voice at last. 'Solutions to what?'

'The flesh-being is impudent,' whispered Erato, 'interrupting a Sentinel.'

'I don't even know what impudent means,' I retorted.

'The child is simply expressing curiosity,' Adi said quickly. 'He is eager for information. Traits he has in common with all his kind . . . and with the Swarm.'

Reboot, the giant camel-spider thing, considered, then nodded its misshapen head. 'The human juvenile's brainwaves seem very basic.'

Thanks, I thought.

'Has he been translated effectively and in full, Scout?'

'Of course,' said Adi.

'Translated?' I asked her. 'You mean, my words, so the Sentinels can understand me?'

Adi looked troubled and turned again to Reboot. 'Full species translation may not be necessary, Sentinel.'

'Tell it we weren't in distress when we sent the Arecibo message,' I urged her. 'We don't need saving.'

Klikker clicked its jaws. 'Flesh-beings should know nothing of our purpose.'

'I pretty much don't,' I admitted. 'Why are you so bothered about helping humans anyway? We must seem like specks of nothing to you.'

'We recognise the value of all organic beings, and the environments that permit them to evolve,' said Erato. 'Worlds like your Earth are the cradles from which we will gain further knowledge to strengthen the Swarm.'

'The Arecibo message showed us your physical form and its chemical composition,' Reboot went on. 'That your population numbered four-point-three billion.'

'And in the fifty years since sending, the human flesh-being population has almost doubled,' Klikker added.

'Such growth places the resources of Earth under serious pressure.' Reboot loomed over me. 'Your world is dying,' it said, in a voice surprisingly soft for a giant mutant camel spider. 'It has passed the tipping point of being able to recover from the environmental damage your race had caused. What intelligent beings *wouldn't* cry out to the stars in distress.'

'But we didn't mean to,' I said, fear grabbing at my mind. 'We . . . we can sort out our own problems.'

'No, Danny,' said Adi. 'You cannot. Humanity is too divided. You are incapable of working together to make change.'

'And you must not be allowed to destroy a world that harbours life,' Reboot rumbled. 'The Earth can endure for four billion more years before your sun expands to engulf it.'

'Plenty of time for more intelligent life forms to evolve and contribute to our Hive,' Erato noted. 'So, since humanity refuses to take the drastic steps needed to preserve its future . . . the Swarm must take them instead.'

I stared at the horrible spider thing. 'What steps?' I almost whispered, not sure I wanted to hear the answer.

Reboot's mandibles twitched. 'We will harvest what little knowledge you can give us now and give life on Earth another chance.'

'We will translate your species into waveforms like ourselves,' Klikker explained. 'When your species is translated into digital information and your bodies eradicated, you will have no physical form, so you will no longer *need* a planet.'

I could hardly take in what I was hearing. 'You're going to turn the human race into a swarm?' The thought was horrible, but I could also see how it made total sense to them. They had already evolved from flesh into pure thought.

For them it was a logical next step. For the human race – game over.

'Please,' I said, feeling sick to my virtual stomach. 'You can't do this.'

'Of course we can, child.' Reboot seemed puzzled. 'You know that we have the necessary technology.'

'But you don't have the *right*!' I shouted. 'You can't just go around the universe choosing who gets to be a flesh-being and who's a digiscan without even telling them.'

'But without intervention, your species will soon go

extinct,' said Klikker. 'Is it not better that your knowledge is harvested and shared with the Swarm? That way the essence of the human race will endure.'

'Survival is all,' Reboot assured me. 'Given time, the human Swarm will adjust. And one day it may benefit from the wisdom of the race that arises to replace you.'

I rounded on Adi. 'You knew this was coming,' I said. 'You knew, but you never said!'

'Naturally, Scout knew,' said Erato. 'Scout was to prepare for our arrival. Work that our agents are now undertaking, since Scout has failed.'

'No.' Adi glowered at the giant spider soldiers. '"Scout" has not failed. "Scout" only says there is a better way.' She took my hand. 'The children of Earth hold the hope for the planet's redemption. This one before you already takes steps to protect his world. He understands the need to care for *all* life on his planet – as do a great many of his kind. I sought to understand them . . . because I wish to work *with* them to save their world.' She smiled at me. 'Work with them as a flesh-being myself.'

The Sentinels stared at her, balefully, through their spider eyes.

'I will change the humans' behaviour,' Adi said, 'make them see the error of their ways. Reduce their numbers and increase their knowledge. Give me just twenty-five Earth years – the same time it took us to reach their world. If you judge then that I have failed in this mission, then, very well. I will translate the human race into the Swarm myself.'

The Sentinels retreated – in shock, I thought, at first – but then they huddled, conferring in low, incomprehensible tones. I stared at Adi, shocked and scared. Was this a trick she was playing, a way to stop the entire human race from streaming into endless ones and zeroes? Or did she truly want to take power for herself?

What did you expect? a voice inside me cried. I could feel the ambition and longing in her. Adi looked like a girl my age, but she was *alien*. The alien equivalent of a worker bee dreaming it could be queen.

Now she saw me looking at her. She gave me a smile. I didn't return it.

'You used me, Adi,' I whispered. 'I risked my life for you . . . and for what? For you to rule the world?'

'I would rule it well! Better than your present leaders . . .' She broke off, her image glitching. She clutched at her temples, looking dizzy. 'No. Oh, no.'

'Scout's request is denied,' Reboot announced. 'Scout has become contaminated by alien code.'

'Scout has grown illogical,' Klikker agreed. 'Irrational. Emotional.'

'Scout must be purged of these weaknesses,' hissed Erato. 'Scout's code will be unravelled. Stripped bare. Re-engineered.'

'No!' Adi screamed, her form flickering. 'Don't make me go back to . . . to *sameness*.'

'Sameness brings unity,' said Reboot calmly. 'Unity brings peace and strength.'

'It brings stagnation!' Adi spat. 'Let me live. Let me *be*!' She looked at me, eyes wide and desperate. 'Danny, I'm sorry. I didn't want this. You must trust me!'

I turned my back on her, and then cringed as Erato scuttled closer to me. 'This child is the first human to be digiscanned. Let him be isolated, all thought processes suspended, until he can rejoin his own race . . . when they are part of the Swarm.'

'I told Adi already,' I said, 'humans won't work in a swarm! Think of all the babies, or old people whose brains have gone fuzzy, all the different beliefs we have—'

'The individual will no longer exist,' Reboot told me. 'An infant has a great capacity to learn. A mind shrunken with age still has knowledge locked inside. In the Swarm, all may contribute, regardless of age or status or ability. Humanity will be brought together in a state of connection. You will have no conflict, because you will own nothing, need nothing, desire nothing. You will become engines of thought, directed by the Hive and controlled by our logic.'

'Directed? Controlled?' I shouted. 'Like slaves!' But I could feel my own body glitch and flicker now, as Adi's was doing, as a digital storm began to blow up inside of me. 'Please . . . don't . . . ! Adi?'

'Hold on, Danny!' Adi shouted. 'You must hold on.'

'No good . . .' I closed my digital eyes as razor-sharp

wires seemed to pull through them. 'Can't stop Sentinels . . . Too strong.'

'Think of Jamila!' I could hear Adi back inside my head. 'Think of playing *Breakout Saturn* together for hours, pushing Maxima Layne through each level . . .' She gasped, as whatever Reboot and the rest were doing to her went deeper. 'Think of how desperately you wanted to beat those last three end-of-level bosses . . . *Think of that!*'

Adi had said it was my mind doing the translating, but I sensed she'd made the Sentinels look this way to make me want to fight them. But it was no use. The crimson void was growing darker, my senses growing dimmer as Klikker, Reboot and Erato began to power me down. 'I . . . can't complete . . . those levels . . . without Jamila . . .'

'Of course you can't,' cried Adi. 'Think of how Jamila would creep back into Munday Mansion! Think of SWIMMER . . .'

'SWIMMER,' I echoed, the same word Adi had made me focus on before. *Secret Window Into Mundays' Mansion, Emergency Route.* Yeah, Jam would go home and then take the emergency exit to join me, and together we'd smash those levels . . .

But no. I was alone, everything was fading.

All I could think of was the last time me and Jamila played *Breakout Saturn* – that first night that Adi came through.

Adi screamed, 'Think of Jamila!'

That night when Maxima Layne ran and let her loyal lieutenant fall to the spiders. The night that Jamila got me killed.

And the darkness closed in.

CHAPTER FIFTEEN
LONG WAY OUT

Is it just me, or do those little moments of defeat stick in your head more than any moments of triumph? They eat at you. You go over them and wish you'd done things differently. I hate how I obsess over them.

But you know, weirdly, I reckon that's what kept me holding on in the Sentinels' storm – as they tried to strip me down to bare data – and kept me conscious just a few vital seconds longer.

Cos I remembered Jamila's smile that night she got me killed as she told me, '*I'll make it up to you, some day.*'

And then, the pain stopped. And in the darkness, in front of me, a square of light appeared and, through it, I saw her. Jamila, striking Maxima Layne's heroic pose with hands on hips and one leg hooked behind the other.

'Danny!' Jamila yelled. 'What the actual . . . ? Where are we, what is this?'

Jamila was there!

She was framed against the light, poised to come through, like I was in my room and she was out on the ledge. Only this time I knew that she was safe and I was outside, so close to falling.

I had to get to her.

Gritting my teeth, I staggered towards her. The light was soft like a nightlight, warm against the chill of the darkness all around. I reached out my digital fingers, afraid my palm would pass right through her.

But her fingers caught mine. 'DANNY? Oh, my days, I never thought I'd reach you . . .' And she pulled me closer, into the light.

And the light was moving, and we were moving with it. Travelling at the speed of light.

'I'm dreaming,' I groaned. 'Got to be. Or else I'm crazy. I'm still stuck in the Swarm. I'm imagining all this. You're not real, you're—'

'Danny, shut up! We're whizzing through who-knows-what and who-knows-where and the only reason I'm not completely freaking my head off right now is cos I'm neck-deep in shock, and I *think* I'm dressed as Maxima Layne and purple stretch pants are not a good look, so let's just try to keep things chill . . .' Jamila was still holding my hand as we sailed on in the light. 'And, yeah, I know it's weird I'm holding your hand but that's not the weirdest thing going on is it? So it's cool if I keep holding on. Yeah?'

'Yeah,' I told her, and I told myself too. *Yeah, keep holding on. Just hold on.*

I closed my eyes and still the soft light shone on as we went. And slowly my thoughts, and the fragments of memory from the storm in the Swarm pieced themselves back together.

'How'd you get here, Jam?' I whispered.

'I'm not even sure,' said Jamila. 'Turns out there was a trace of Adi in my phone from when we met.'

Yeah, I thought, *she does that.*

Jamila went on: 'Anyway, just before you were snarled up and taken away, Adi used that trace of her to warn me you were in danger. Life and death. That I was your only chance, and I had to get to this warehouse by the river where she had this weird home-made machine that makes bodies out of brainwaves . . . which can do the opposite, too.'

I stared at her, marvelling. 'You worked out how to turn the bodyprinter into a digiscan thing?'

'Huh? Shut up, course I didn't!' Jamila frowned. 'I just stuck my SIM card into the machine, like she'd messaged. Adi had done something to it. It sorted everything for me.'

'Maybe,' I said. 'But you *risked* everything for me. I don't know just what it was you did, but you came after us. You might just have saved me and Adi.'

'Sure, Maxima Layne's got nothing on Jamila al-Sufi,' she scowled, passing off the praise. 'Well *you're* here. But Adi . . .'

'She's here with us right now,' I assured her. 'Otherwise you really would be freaking your face off, and we wouldn't be seeing each other . . .' I raised my voice. 'Would we, Adi?'

Like a ghost, Adi formed between the two of us, see-through arms draped around our shoulders. She looked tired and shaken, but there was strength in her smile.

'What the hell happened back there?' I asked her. 'How'd we get out?'

'I knew that the Swarm would summon me back sometime. There's no way I could get away with going rogue,' Adi said. 'I hoped to use my own digiscanner to travel there in radiowaves – so I buried an exit algorithm in the code generator – a way for me to get back to Earth again.'

Jamila looked blank. 'You did what?'

As best I could, I translated: 'I reckon that when you were changed from flesh and blood into digital, Jam, you smuggled Adi's escape route into the Swarm with you!'

'That's right,' Adi agreed. 'The Guardian could not detect it because a "back way" in and out of the Swarm's digital world is not malicious, or dangerous or a weapon. It is merely an idea. An idea that would never occur to the Sentinels.'

'Cos they're all logic and rational,' I realised. 'They'd

never expect another human to come charging in and out through a window. Pretty smart, Adi.'

'It was *your* thinking of Jamila that drew her to us,' said Adi, smiling at the way we were still holding hands. 'That bond of friendship between you made it possible, a further concept the Sentinels could not understand.'

'What, and you think *you* understand friendship?' Now we were out and clear I felt my anger start to return. 'You almost got me killed, Adi.'

'I saved you!'

'Jamila saved me – you only used us to make your plan work and save yourself.' I shrugged off her ghostly arm. 'That's your idea of friendship. Using people. Like you used me to keep the drones off your back. Like you used me to learn about the world because you figured I'd be up for changing it . . . in a way that suits *you*.'

'Danny, what are you talking about?' Jamila looked anxious and I couldn't blame her. 'What's been happening?'

So I told her what had gone down, and about the fate

that was facing our world – the world that the Swarm wanted to make human-free.

'But . . .' Jamila looked terrified. 'But that can't happen. Can it?'

'It can if we can't stop it.' I looked at Adi. 'The Swarm's gonna come after us, isn't it?'

'They have no need to,' said Adi. 'Swarm agents were already at work on the Earth before we left. By the time we return, their work will be nearly complete.'

'What d'you mean, *by the time we return*?' asked Jamila. 'You know I have no clue how long we've been gone.'

'Your human idea of time is an illusion, based on the spin of your world as it circles your sun,' Adi told her. 'Now we are radio waves, passing through your solar system.'

'So it won't take us long to get back, right?' I said. Travelling this way was kind of like being in a dream. 'How long has this trip taken?'

'The Swarm is in holding orbit far beyond the Kuiper belt,' Adi reminded me. 'Even moving at the speed of light, it takes more than ten Earth days for us to reach the Swarm, and over ten again to return. And then there was the time we spent inside the Swarm . . .'

'What?' I yelled. 'You mean we'll have been missing from home for *three weeks*?'

'My mum's head will have blown up with worry,' groaned Jamila. 'Oh, my days . . .'

I supposed even *my* mum might have noticed me missing by now. But that wasn't my biggest concern. 'If the Swarm's work is nearly complete, how long will it take the Swarm to start sucking up everyone's brainwaves? And what happens to the human race then?'

'I don't know,' Adi said. 'I told you, I am the advance scout, not a Swarm agent. Once I have explored a world and mapped the way to travel through its native technology, my mission is complete and I share the information with the Swarm.'

I stared at her. 'You never wanted to know? Never thought to ask?'

'You spend so much of your life on your PlayStation,' said Adi, 'but do you grasp how each circuit functions?

Of course not.' She shrugged. 'The knowledge was not relevant to my function. It had no value to me.'

'Well, now it does,' I said. 'Find out, Adi! Please!'

'Of course, I can access the information . . .' But Adi trailed off and I saw sudden fear twist her perfect features. 'There's nothing there.'

'What?' asked Jamila.

'My connection to the Swarm has been severed.' Adi seemed in shock. 'Cast out from the Hive Mind. I am . . . I am . . .'

I frowned. 'You all right, Adi?'

'I am . . . *separate*.' She stared at me, uncomprehending. 'Alone.'

I opened my mouth, though whether to object or agree I wasn't sure. But then I felt something tugging at me. Not at my body – I knew that was just a projection. This was like something pulling at my soul. Or at my radio waves at least. 'Uh, Adi . . . ?'

Adi blinked, distracted suddenly from her crisis. 'We are nearing the Earth,' Adi said. 'The influence you can feel is my bodyprinter, drawing our signals from space like a lightning rod conducts lightning. Ready to make us flesh-beings once again.'

'Back to that dingy dump of a warehouse, then,' said Jamila, and Adi nodded.

As the pull grew stronger, I said, 'Wait. There's only one coffin thing and three of us. How do we get back?'

'We will be stacked in a queue,' said Adi, 'and printed one after the other.'

Jamila shrugged at me. 'Like the jobs queue on a paper printer.'

'Yeah, but hang on,' I said, anxiety levels rising. 'Where are our bodies now?'

'Deconstructed,' said Adi simply.

'Decon-*what*-ed?' Jamila stared. 'Mine too?'

Adi nodded. 'The same devices that harvest the brainwaves implant a physical destructor code into the body. When triggered, it deconstructs the organic material at a subcellular level.'

'Right,' I agreed, 'but in words that make sense?'

'Your bodies have been turned into small piles of chemical residue,' Adi said.

Me and Jamila screamed together, 'WHAT?'

'Don't worry. An exact copy of the body is stored at the moment of upload,' Adi went on calmly. 'The organic building blocks of the human form – like carbon, hydrogen, nitrogen – are easy to synthesise. Human beings are pretty simple organisms. You will be recreated exactly as you were.'

I remembered the news story on my phone. 'What about those missing parents in Manchester,' I said. 'The piles of grit left behind and the tracker-bot drones outside.'

'I suppose the Swarm agents had to test the physical destructor code ahead of using it on humanity,' Adi said.

'And no one's bringing *them* back,' said Jamila. 'The Swarm killed them.'

'Not killed – harvested and awaiting translation. Anyway, over a million humans are killed by other humans each year in traffic accidents,' Adi said calmly. 'A hundred and fifty thousand people around the world die each day. What difference do two more make to you? Were they . . . *close* to you?'

'That's not the point! They were *parents*. They had a

child. A child who is now an orphan. What if those two lives were mine and Jamila's?' I demanded.

Adi flinched and looked away, her frown fixed as if in deep concentration. 'I am bringing you back to life,' she said finally. 'And because of our journey time, you will have lived for approximately twenty-two days without aging.' She held up her thumbs. 'Win!'

But I hardly heard her as a sudden panic bit my brain. 'There may be a copy of you and Jam in your bodyprinter, Adi, but I never used the thing, did I? I was zapped up from the Swarm agents' bodyprinter. That's where *my* scan is stored! Probably right in the middle of their base. I'm gonna come back to life right in front of them!'

'Adi, you can do something about that, yeah?' Jamila turned to her, wild-eyed. 'You came through with him, so you can fix this.'

Adi looked sad.

'She can't,' I said. 'The agents would get us both.'

'Then we'll come and get you,' Jamila told me, trying to force a smile, though tears were in her eyes. 'Look,

I went ten zillion miles to come and get you out last time, this'll be a piece of . . .'

Her voice faded. Adi and Jamila seemed to streak away from me, nothing left but trails of light. Then they were gone too and all I knew was dark. Absolute dark.

I don't know how long I was held in nothingness, but slowly I became aware of a deep, penetrating hum.

I was no longer weightless, no longer free. I had to be back inside the Swarm agents' bodyprinter. Sensation sparked inside me as I began to be remade. I felt my heart start. Fingers twitched and fear dug in like claws. I felt like sand in an hourglass, drawn out by gravity. Falling into familiar forms but still trapped.

I imagined the Swarm agents watching as their bodyprinter sparked into life. Their eyes glowing in their misshapen faces. The more solid I became, the harder my fear took hold, and when the door of the cabinet hissed open I moaned with terror.

But it was only Adi looking in at me. She smiled as I staggered out, placed her hands on my shoulders to steady me.

We were back in the old, abandoned warehouse. I was going to ask how come, but my brain was suddenly screaming as it wrestled with weight and balance and breathing. I could see and feel my body, my clothes, and yes, everything seemed just as it was before – right down to the chicken pox scar on my arm, the feel of my tongue on my wonky incisor, the grass stain on the knee of my jeans, even coins in the pocket – only suddenly I felt so *small*, like a tiny prison pressing in on my spirit. Was this how astronauts felt coming back to Earth? My heart thump, the wheeze and drag of my lungs, blinking to moisturise my eyes – my body felt like a chain gang at work, straining to hold together as one.

'The feeling will pass,' Adi told me, as if reading my noisy thoughts.

'How are we here?' I said hoarsely. 'I wasn't ever scanned into your magic box.'

Adi shrugged. 'I retrieved your bio-code from the Agents' digiscanner.'

'But you said you'd been cut off from the Swarm?'

'I have.' She looked downcast. 'But they haven't cut

me off from our native network here on Earth.' She paused. 'It's only a matter of time. Now I've used the bodyprinter, the Swarm agents will know that I have returned. We must not linger here.'

'Where's Jamila?' I asked, looking round.

'Still waiting to come through,' said Adi, turning back to the lashed-up bodyprinter and tapping commands. 'Now you are complete, she can be reproduced too.'

But as Adi spoke, I could hear scuffles on the steps outside the warehouse. There was a clang as the door was smashed in and suddenly figures in black hazard suits were pouring in with all kinds of weird tech, like *Ghostbusters* had gone over to the military.

I stared dumbly. We'd travelled to the far side of the solar system and back only to be caught in some stinky old warehouse. I didn't have the energy to fight any more.

My time was up.

CHAPTER SIXTEEN
NOWHERE TO RUN

I looked at Adi. 'Swarm agents?'

'No,' said Adi. 'Human beings.'

There were twelve of them, standing like soldiers but staring like scientists. Some held silver wands linked to backpacks, others had cameras and recording devices. They scattered through the warehouse, aiming their gear this way and that. 'Space is clear!' one of them called, the voice crackling over a loudspeaker. 'Empty rooms.'

Still adjusting to being a thing of flesh and blood again, I held up my hands. 'Don't shoot,' I said.

'Please don't be alarmed.' A woman stepped through to the front of the crowd and addressed Adi. 'I am Doctor Araminta Pearce, Director of the British Special Cybersecurity Unit. Step away from that machine and tell me who's in charge.'

Adi stared at her. 'What is here is mine.'

Pearce wasn't having it. 'How are you involved?' she demanded. 'Who brought you here?'

'Uh, I'm Danny Munday,' I began. 'You've got to listen to me—'

'We know who you are,' said Pearce, jerking her head towards me. 'What's been happening here?'

'You'd never believe me.' I closed my eyes. 'How do you know who I am?'

'Your mother reported you as missing shortly after intense bursts of radiation were detected in this area. We've identified this building as the original focus point.' She looked back at Adi and a flint edge hardened her voice. 'So answer me. How are you involved and who brought you here?'

Adi scowled, her palm pressed firmly against the machine. '*You*, Doctor Pearce, are acting like a total douche.'

I groaned, and hissed, 'No, Adi!'

'Do you have any idea how serious the situation is, "Adi"?' Pearce inquired. 'You will come with us to a secure facility and submit to questioning.'

'Maybe it's best,' I said to Adi. 'This could be our chance to warn them about the Swarm . . .'

Adi laughed. 'These little fools can't stop what's coming, Danny.'

'All right, we've wasted enough time.' Pearce gestured to her team to close in on us. 'You'll both come with us.'

'No,' said Adi, taking my hand and pulling me away from the bodyprinter towards the corner of the warehouse. The Cybersecurity Unit fanned out around us, making sure we were well covered.

'There's nowhere to run,' Pearce warned us.

'Not true.' Adi shook her head sadly. 'For as long as is left, there's *only* running.'

Without warning the bodyprinter blew apart in a haze of violet flame. The explosion shook the warehouse, blew brick dust from the walls. Dr Pearce and her ghostbusters were blasted across the room as sparks of energy lashed out like electric whipcords.

'Jamila!' I screamed. 'Adi, if she was in there . . . Adi?'

She'd been protecting us both from the electrical storm with some kind of invisible shield. Now, as the blast died away, Adi staggered back against the wall, looking exhausted.

'Adi?' I grabbed her by the shoulders. 'Where's Jamila . . .'

'It's all right,' Adi said, woozily. 'I'm sorry. My energenes are not yet fully generated.'

'Did you know the bodyprinter was gonna blow, Adi?' I checked on Dr Pearce and the others. They were still breathing but knocked out cold. 'Well?'

'Yes, I did,' she said. 'The Swarm agents sent a negative pulse through the network. They must have realised I had just operated the machine and hoped to damage me by its destruction, so I would be easier to capture. We must leave here, Danny.'

'What about Jamila? You said she was all right, but she hadn't come through and now there's nowhere *to* come through. So where is she?'

'Remember, I told you – an exact copy is stored at the moment of upload. Jamila's code is in the system, Danny,' Adi said. 'But her days of flesh-being are over. We cannot reprint her now.'

'What?' I stared at her. 'She can't be gone. You just told me it was all right!'

'Well, it is. Her digitised brainwaves are hidden securely, even from the Swarm. Part of the code I wrote for our escape erased all trace of her trespass.' Adi shrugged. 'But I will tell you where to look. And once you're translated into digital being, you will know where to find her.'

'So, what, I'm meant to cheer?' I recoiled from her. 'My best friend . . . and she could be anywhere. Gone from this world.'

'You will be together again soon enough,' said Adi. 'In the human Swarm.'

'Shut up!' I couldn't believe that she was acting so calmly while I was shaking with anger. 'You just don't care, do you? We don't want to be a part of the stupid Swarm, we want to be *us*.'

'You know that humanity's behaviour makes that impossible.'

'No – *Swarm* behaviour makes it impossible!'

'Do you think that dooming your planet's future,

condemning billions to a slow, miserable death, is a superior outcome to living eternally as a part of the Swarm? If the Sentinels had allowed me to rule you, perhaps I could have helped make the changes you seem incapable of making yourselves, but since my wishes have been denied . . .'

I wanted to yell and shout and cry like a kid. Instead I just buried my face in my hands. 'Why did you bother to come back here, if joining the Swarm is all we can do?'

'I want what I have wanted all along,' Adi said. 'To experience flesh-being in full for as long as I can. To know physical life. To be . . . *me*.' She paused. 'Come with me, Danny?'

'What?' I took my hands away and looked at her. 'Just forget the end of the world is coming and go party with you?'

'There is so much I want to experience.' Adi's eyes were shining. 'Thin air in the mountains. The heat of the desert. To feel waves lap at my feet. To travel through the air in silly, slow machines as you do . . .' She laughed. 'I want to eat pizza all around the world, Danny!'

She sounded like a little girl the night before her birthday. 'A big adventure, huh,' I muttered. 'Before "flesh-being" is over for ever.'

'That's right. Please, Danny. I want to experience all I can. You must do too—'

'How about *saving* all you can?' I cut in. 'You can think of a way to get Jamila back, stop the Swarm from doing this, show them that your plan would work. My generation, we *do* want change. You don't even have to rule us – we could work *with* you. There's still hope!'

'No. It's too late, Danny. So, I must leave.' She reached out for my hand. 'Come with me.'

'I can't!' I protested. 'My mum will be going crazy worrying about me—'

'I can make her forget,' said Adi. 'It will be easy . . .'

'Easy!' I shook my head disgusted. 'What else will you do that's easy – make me forget Mum so I go with you? Make me forget the Swarm even exists so I don't bring you down?'

Adi nodded eagerly. 'I can do this if you'd like me to?'

I just stared at her, not even believing how badly she didn't get it.

'Oh, and that picture you made in the sky of you and me, when we pressed our faces together,' she went on. 'I want to try that. I want to make it real.'

'When people kiss it means they like each other,' I said slowly. 'And I don't like you, Adi. You're just code in cosplay. You know *nothing* about being human.'

She looked confused. 'Danny?'

'Go on, then, get out of here. Go tick the things off your bucket list and have a good time till the time runs out.' I bunched my fists and shouted. '*Go.*'

And she did. Adi turned from me and walked slowly to the door.

Then she faded out of sight.

I was alone in the warehouse with an unconscious cybersecurity unit. I guessed I'd better get going too. I felt like a baby but I really just wanted to see my mum and dad, and give them a hug. I wiped the wetness from my eyes and lingered for a minute by the wreckage of the bodyprinter.

As I gathered myself together, something shiny on the scorched floor caught my eye. There, amongst the charred wreckage of the bodyprinter, was what looked like a SIM card. I remembered Jamila's voice in my head as she'd explained how she'd shrugged off her body and come into the Swarm: 'Adi had done something to it. It sorted everything for me.'

Something. Everything. Nothing.

I remembered that last night Jam and I played *Breakout Saturn*. 'It's my turn to play Maxima next,' I'd said, 'and I'm totally gonna get you killed . . .'

You ever wish you could go back in time and unsay stuff?

Someone on the floor stirred and groaned, coming to. It was time to go. What could I do to save the human race from extinction? Nothing. I was done. I just wanted to get home and see my mum before the end of the world.

I pushed the SIM card in my pocket and left the warehouse. Kept my head down. Didn't look back.

CHAPTER SEVENTEEN
BLUE MUNDAY

It was a mega anticlimax, coming home. I'd lost my phone – it hadn't reformed along with the rest of me, so I guess the Swarm agents took it, or it fell out of my pocket, or something. So I couldn't phone ahead.

All the way back on the bus, I was picturing a mahoosive reunion with my mum, tears and snot and promises of immediate zip-wire adventures and – no – I really *didn't* have to catch up on the last three weeks' schoolwork. Maybe Dad had come back from Hawaii to comfort my mourning mother, and they'd both yell my name as I came through the door and Dad wouldn't even tell me to take my shoes off before I traipsed mud everywhere . . .

I've been gone a long time, I thought, *but I've come back a new person.*

Literally.

But the house was dark when I got there. No one in. The lights were on at Jamila's. I wondered how Jam's family must be feeling, not knowing where she was. How could I ever face them again, knowing that her not being here was my fault. I felt so deep down and helpless and afraid. I knew that Dr Pearce would come looking for me. And even if she and her team believed my story, Adi was right – there was nothing they could do against the Swarm.

I checked Mum wasn't asleep anywhere inside. But it looked like no one had been there for days. Full of nerves, I tried phoning Mum from the landline. She wasn't picking up. Of course she wasn't.

I went to the fridge and almost threw up at the stink inside. I mean, worse than usual, there were things actually rotting and the only milk turned halfway to blue cheese.

Maybe I should surrender to Dr Pearce right now, I thought darkly. *The food's got to be better.*

I opened a bag of crisps and gazed around the tip that was our kitchen. I'd missed three weeks and two days; it didn't seem possible. Poor Mum, I thought guiltily, imagining what she must've gone through. Maybe she'd gone away to stay with friends? She wouldn't think to leave a note because after all this time, why would she be expecting me back? I'd disappeared.

On the table there were web-news printouts and pages cut from the newspaper. They all seemed to be about problems with Wi-Fi signals messing up across Europe and the USA regardless of supplier . . . UK phone networks had unexplained outages . . . 6G masts were being blamed for a rash of headaches in the populations of India and China. There were even a couple of reports of radio telescopes malfunctioning in Australia and Peru, the huge dishes shifting position, apparently of their own accord.

I had a better idea who had made it happen.

As I picked up the most recent pages, which were three days old, I found Mum's phone underneath. A pang of worry cut right through me. Wherever she'd gone, Mum had left her mobile behind. Who did that? It was dead. I plugged it in, hoping I'd find some clue on it to why she'd gone.

Lost in thought, I almost jumped out of my skin

when the landline rang. It was an international number, and I picked up. 'Yes?'

'Danny?' Dad's voice sounded so loud in my ear. 'Danny, that's you, isn't it?'

'It's me, Dad,' I said, swallowing back tears; now was not the time. 'Dad, I—'

'Where the hell have you been?' Dad bellowed. 'Your mum and me, we've been out of our minds!'

'Dad, I—'

'I flew over to see her, praying you'd come back to us. We've been sick with worry, Danny!'

'Yeah,' I tried again, 'but Dad—'

He was in full flow. 'I only went back again to Hawaii because I felt so useless. I thought work might help to keep my mind off things, but then the radio telescopes went down . . .'

'Yours too?' I broke in sharply. 'Like the ones in Australia and South America?'

'Yes.' He sounded surprised that I should know. 'Yes, the dishes angled down even beyond the set range of the couplings. Shouldn't be possible, but . . .'

My dad gets easily distracted; Mum says that's why he left in the first place. 'Dad, I'm home but Mum's not here. When did you last speak to her?'

'I've been trying to get through to her the last couple of days. Perhaps she's staying with friends . . .' He paused for a second. 'What happened, Danny? Are you all right?'

What could I say? *Hey Dad, forget the 'scopes, I've travelled through space myself now. I'll tell you all about it.*

Nah. Maybe not.

I just said I'd been caught up in some weird local fast radio burst and my memory was messed up . . . that I'd been found by the cybersecurity unit and I was fine, but where was Mum? And Dad said he would be on the next flight back to see me. I was glad. But it's like thirty hours or more by plane from Kailua-Kona to London, with the stopover and stuff; Dad wouldn't get up here till the day after tomorrow.

My mind had a dizzying flashback to travelling through the void, moving so fast it felt like time was standing still. Adi could've covered the distance in less than a heartbeat.

I was too tired to be mad at her. I just felt sad and heavy.

'Hope you're living your best life, Adi,' I muttered.

I took Mum's phone and the charger upstairs, kicked off my shoes and my jeans and laid on my bed for the first time in weeks – well, for the first time ever in this body. I turned on the TV, wanting the comfort of normal life, trying not to picture Jamila's empty room on the other side.

The streaming news came on. And it was all bad.

There were reports of massive electrical power outages across major cities. In Japan the stock market had completely crashed because of software glitches, causing financial chaos. Two satellites had collided in space – one Chinese, one American – each blaming the other for faulty commands from the ground.

Maybe it was coincidence, I thought. Or, as I watched on grimly, maybe not.

Cos there were other stories. More people gone missing – a Norwegian prince among them – with only an odd patch of wet silt left behind. In Sydney, a car had gone out of control and driven off a bridge, but the driver's body could not be found. In Miami a cruise liner had crashed straight into harbour with not a soul aboard – over two thousand passengers and crew missing, the decks scattered with a strange, crimson gravel. In Russia a military fighter landed on autopilot with no sign of the pilot and no ejection.

'So many mysteries,' the news anchor said with a resigned, what're-you-gonna-do smile. But they weren't mysteries to me.

Swarm agents, I thought grimly. The quickest way to travel digitally would be through our tech – that could be causing the mess-ups. Maybe they were already gathering brainwaves. And the people vanishing – more tests? Glitches in the systems? Physical destructor codes accidentally triggered too soon?

'It's all real,' I said out loud. 'All really happening.'

I switched off the TV, got up and flopped down on to Mum's unmade bed instead. Soon I'd fallen into deep and dreamless sleep.

I woke up with a jerk around 5 a.m. at the sound of Mum's phone buzzing. I looked at the screen but it was just an alert from some dumb game she played. But now the phone was awake and unlocked it showed me a list of unanswered calls. Dad had phoned her lots, and Araminta Pearce from Cybersecurity and a couple of her friends from the street. I saw Mum had messaged some of her colleagues at the Jodrell radiotelescope, asking if they were OK, and what was the deal with 'the quantum computer set-up' that was taking everyone away from real work twenty-four seven.

The last message she'd sent was to her boss, three days ago: *Finally, I get the summons to join Masterplan QC, lol! About the only project still running. Would like to talk through with you when I come in. Thanks, L.'*

Maybe Mum had moved into one of the flats on-site at her work, normally used by overseas visitors? I felt fresh twinges of guilt: perhaps living here without me had become too much for her. But why had she left her phone behind?

'Masterplan QC,' I said aloud. 'Got to be QC for quantum computer?'

I had no idea what one was, and a quick web search

left my head running for cover. What I did grasp was that quantum computing was meant to solve supercomplex problems that regular computers couldn't handle – and solve them superfast, too.

Why would something like that be needed at a radio telescope?

I tried phoning Mum's work – it was early, sure, but I knew plenty of staff there worked night shifts. No one picked up. I tried her boss's number direct. No answer, but then I wasn't really expecting one. My head was buzzing with premonitions of doom. People acting weirdly, Mum going AWOL, new, crazy advanced computers being built – and all connected to the place where the Swarm had first come through on Earth.

I felt so lonely. *Oh, Jam*, I thought miserably. *Why aren't you here to talk to about all this . . . ?*

Then I had a sudden spark of inspiration. Of course – Adi had sneaked herself out into the world on a data stick and from there out through the Wi-Fi . . . What if something of Jamila was still on that SIM card I'd taken from the wreck of the bodyprinter?

With sweaty hands I removed Mum's SIM and swapped it for Jamila's. Then, heart bouncing madly, I waited for something to come through. Some sign that she was out there.

But what if it was only the ghost of her – traces left behind in the SIM's silicon chip, like a recorded message, texting me random words? I put down the phone, creeping myself out and feeling horribly alone.

The sun slowly rose but no message came through.

Around 8 a.m. I decided to get up and go back to my own room and fire up the PlayStation. Gaming was the only way I knew to switch off my head and my troubles and just lose myself. The hiss of the cooling fans was soothing as I waited for *Breakout Saturn* to load. Jam might not be around just now, but Captain Maxima Layne, Fearless Queen of the Spaceways was always there when needed. Right now, I badly needed to vent my frustration on the evil Spidroid ranks. Captain Max gave her signature salute and started tearing through the arachnids, zapping them out of existence left, right and centre. It was pretty good therapy and made me feel a little closer to Jamila, wherever she might be.

Until the game froze, mid-Maxima melee attack. 'Oh, my days!' I cried.

And on the screen, Maxima Layne crossed her arms and narrowed her eyes at me. 'Oi,' she said, blowing away the bad guys with one puff of breath. 'That's my line, Danny-boy.'

'Huh?' I dropped the controller in shock.

It didn't matter. Maxima kept moving anyway.

'Thanks for letting me out through the Wi-Fi,' she said. 'I guess this is how Adi did it.'

'Jam?' I whispered, heart skittering. 'Jamila, is that actually you?'

'Pretty sure,' she agreed. 'I came in here cos . . .'

'Cos why wouldn't you!' I laughed, putting my hands against the screen. 'Oh, Jam, I thought— Wait.' I looked down in panic. 'You can't see out of that screen, can you?'

'Course I can't. No more than Maxima can. Why, you playing in your boxers or something?'

'Um, no,' I lied. 'Oh, Jam, I'm so glad to hear you. I thought you were lost! You're alive!'

'I'm talking to you as a video-game character, you muppet, of course I'm not "alive". And yes, I *am* lost. I remember you, me and Adi zapping through space, but then everything stopped . . .' Jamila paused and Maxima looked cartoon sad with a little black cloud over her head. 'I'm just code now. Just a bunch of information. You wanna know how hard it is to keep track of yourself when you're basically a string of ones and zeroes? That's why I came in here – it's something I know, something I understand.'

I got it. 'Maxima Layne's always been your avatar.'

'Out there . . . it's like . . .' Maxima – I mean, Jamila, or Jamaxima? – shuddered. 'Danny, d'you ever see *Ralph Breaks the Internet?*'

'Sure, as a kid.'

'Well, I guess I always imagined the Web to be something like that. But guess what. It isn't.' She moved closer to the screen. 'It's terrible, Danny. All . . . data and darkness. It's like you're a drop of water in an ocean the size of Jupiter, and Jupiter just blew up. It's like you're standing blindfolded in the middle of a motorway while a hundred tornadoes come down on you – like you're gonna get hit or blown away any second. It's—'

'I get it,' I told her. 'You're stuck in the Internet and that's crazy and wrong, totally wrong.'

'Tell me about it,' said Jamaxima. 'And I'm telling you, the cookies you get here don't taste good.'

'We need to find Adi,' I said. 'She'll know what to do.'

'She isn't there now?'

'We had a falling out.' I shrugged. 'Over you.'

'Great,' said Jamaxima, 'so it's my fault, huh?'

'No! It's just . . .' I sighed. 'Oh, Jam, everything is so messed up and I dunno what to do.'

Jamaxima held up her hand. 'I can relate. But I think maybe I can find out where Adi is.'

'You mean, you're gonna just travel around the whole Internet till you find her?'

'There's more than just the Internet out here,' Adi said. 'I guess cos I came through Adi's Swarm circuits, I can listen in on the Swarm network too. And the Swarm, Danny, they've spread pretty much everywhere.'

I felt my mouth turn dry.

'It's like this glowing trail running wireless to pretty much every phone, every laptop and computer and console . . . even cars, Danny. Every way we connect to each other. It's like the Swarm is listening in . . . to everyone. Through everything.'

'This must be what their agents have been doing while we were gone,' I realised.

'Yup,' Jamaxima said. 'What's Adi gonna do about it?'

'Nothing,' I said bitterly. 'She's living it up while she can. She's . . . not coming back.'

'Well she's got to. Or else . . . guess I'm not coming back either.' Jamaxima looked down at her rendered feet.

I put my hand against the screen.

'*Danny.*' She looked up sharply, and the PlayStation whooshed louder as if she were somehow driving it harder. 'Danny, quick. People are coming for you. Two cars are approaching with your address in their satnav. Swarm maybe. You've got to get out of there.'

'What?' I rushed to my window, looked out and swore. A smart black car was pulling up outside.

The door opened and Dr Pearce climbed out, still in

her protective hazard clothing but minus her helmet. Three of her team were with her – like her, clad from neck to toe in black plastic. They started down the path to my front door.

'It's not Swarm, Jamila,' I said, frantically pulling on my jeans. 'It's Cybersecurity. They nearly got me before. I'm gonna split but I'll take Mum's phone.' I shoved my feet into my trainers. 'Get back in the SIM card, stay with me?'

Jamaxima opened her mouth to reply but my screen cut dead and sparks burst from the plug socket. The hiss of the console became a splutter.

There was a crash from downstairs, the front door was smashed in. My outrage that they would just hammer their way into my home quickly gave way to terror. I pushed the phone in my pocket, ran across the landing to the bathroom at the back of the house and shut the door, sliding the bolt across. Then I struggled with the window catch. The stupid thing wouldn't budge. Just as I was ready to pick up the bin and try to smash my way through the frosted pane, the catch gave way and I forced the window open.

Two more of Pearce's team were staring up at me from down below.

Heart sinking, I turned as the bathroom door was smashed open, the bolt tearing away from the door frame. A man and a woman pushed inside and grabbed me, forcing me to my knees.

'Let me go!' I shouted, struggling to get free. 'You can't do this.'

Dr Pearce was standing on the landing, her head tilted to one side. 'You will come with us, Danny Munday,' she said, her voice flat and emotionless. 'To the Swarm.'

'No, please,' I begged her. 'Why does the Swarm want me now? Why?'

'To the Swarm,' Pearce said calmly.

'You're working for them?' Icy chills flooded through my blood and I struggled harder. 'The Swarm's controlling you all?'

'The Swarm,' Pearce said, her eyes like dark holes in an empty head. 'You will come with us to the Swarm.'

CHAPTER EIGHTEEN
DANGER WITHIN

I'd only been to Mum's workplace once. It was a few years back when I was off school sick and she couldn't find anyone to sit with me. I didn't want to go, but the people were kind and showed me round the control room and the enormous Lovell radio telescope. I was blown away by the sheer size of this humungous upturned limpet pointed to the sky – still one of the largest radio telescopes in the world, Mum said. It had been probing the depths of space for over fifty years, listening for weak signals.

Now, here I was being taken to Mum's work again, just as reluctantly. There was this one guy back then who'd been lumbered with me and I remembered he'd said, 'Maybe you'll grow up to be as brilliant as your mum and one day be working here too!' He'd kept saying it, more and more awkwardly. I guess he couldn't think of what else to say to me.

Dr Pearce apparently had the same problem. Sat beside me in the back of her car as we drove through the Jodrell security gates, she kept saying, 'You will come with us to the Swarm,' under her breath. Over and over.

What did the Swarm want from me?

I knew that their power was controlling her mind; I'd seen it happen in town when I'd made those people watch my back. Adi had said the human mind was too murky to control – but I didn't need to be as brilliant as my mum to work out that was one more lie. I guessed the Swarm agents must have come looking for Adi in the warehouse and found Pearce and the Unit there, ready to be enslaved. And it didn't take a genius to work out that Mum's workplace was now being used as the Swarm base: the place where their scout had first come through. Where better? One radio telescope linked to others right the way around the world. Like a mini Internet with links to outer space.

Somehow I didn't think this gang of zombies was

going to give me any kind of a tour. I felt sick, sweaty all over. The worst nerves I'd ever had; I almost felt like I was burning up with a fever. When I saw the great dish of the radio telescope pointing downward instead of up at the stars, like the others in the news feeds and Dad's in Hawaii, my foreboding became at least a five- or sixboding.

What was happening here?

What was going to happen to me?

The car stopped outside a part of the site I'd never seen before. Thick clear plastic strips hung down from a white awning outside a low building, like something infectious had broken out and this was a quarantined area. Outside were arrow signs pointing to CLEANROOM. I knew that was a place where precision tech was made in air free of dust or other particles.

I looked at Pearce. 'Is that where the Swarm keeps its quantum computer?' It was a pretty good guess, I thought, and I hoped she would be shaken by my powerful insight. But all she could say was, 'You will come with us to the Swarm,' and guided me towards the door.

'No thanks,' I said, and yanked my arm free, turning to run. But two more people from the Unit were blocking my way. They grabbed my arms, twisted them behind my back and forced me through the plastic strips into a kind of high-tech waiting room, lit yellow.

Inside my heart leaped. There was Mum, dressed in what she called a bunny suit – plastic coveralls with a matching hood to hide her hair. She was holding more coveralls in her arms.

'Mum!' I shouted. 'Help me!'

She saw me and started forward, reaching out her arms to me. I struggled to break free. But Mum's face was blank and shadowed in the weird lighting. Then I realised she wasn't trying to hug me, she was only holding out the coveralls for me to wear, like I was any other worker going into the cleanroom. She didn't know me.

The Swarm had got her, and to see her that way sent anger burning through me. 'Wake up, Mum!' I shouted. 'It's Danny!'

And for a moment I saw her eyes flicker and real expression steal into her face. *She's coming back!* I thought.

But then a wave of dizziness shook me so hard that I almost fell to my knees. What was wrong with me?

Mum looked down at me and her expression had slipped back to blank. 'Wear the coveralls,' she said quietly. 'Wear the coveralls.'

Trembling, feeling faint, I slowly put on the full outfit. It came with boots and hood built in. Fans were whooshing overhead, purifying the air, but still I was sure that the rapid thud of my heartbeat carried above it.

Once my coverall was in place, a man in matching protective gear stepped forward and grabbed me by the arm. He dragged me from the gowning area through a set of double doors. I caught a last look at Dr Pearce and my mum standing there, calmly watching my struggles. Then the doors swung shut and I was in an entryway that pulsed with sinister light. Jet nozzles in the walls blew gales of purified air, and the man lifted my arms so I was swept clean. I didn't even bother to struggle any more.

It was time to meet whatever was waiting behind the steel door ahead of us. My cold sweat was running set to drown me. Why had I been brought here? What would I find?

Finally the door slid open with a grinding hum, and an arctic blast hit me harder than the air shower. I was staring into a large, sterile room, freezing cold, bathed in an electric glare and with dry ice swirling around above the floor. My eyes were pulled to a huge circle of metal cylinders suspended from a kind of gleaming sci-fi scaffold, bristling with unguessable components.

Each cylinder was etched with rows of circuits threaded together by thousands of skinny wires that looked like angel hair pasta. The air shimmered around the cylinders: shifting shapes and shadows spiralled in the space surrounding the structure before they were sucked inside, like ghostly water down an invisible plughole. And there, suspended in the air above the cylinders, was some kind of bright globe of swirling energy.

The sight chilled me more than the freezing atmosphere. I remembered Adi telling me: 'We developed quantum computers that could combine and magnify the intelligence of our entire civilisation into a single Hive Mind . . .

'And I've just found one,' I whispered, my breath coming out like smoke.

The man pushed me forward, one hand tight on my shoulder. I saw two cabinets, like chest freezers stood vertically, one on either side of the machine. They had keypads and controls on their shiny surfaces. *Digiscanners*, I supposed. This had to be where the Swarm agents had taken me and Adi after we'd lost the duel with them.

And clearly they felt there was unfinished business.

Opposite the sci-fi computer, on the far side of the room, I could see a chunky PC tower and the black eye of a monitor screen shining green characters into the smoky gloom. Two steel-grey figures stood in front of it.

'I'm here,' I called. 'What are you going to do, then? Make me a slave like you did my mum, and her friends, and . . . ?'

I trailed off as the Swarm agents stalked through the coolant smoke towards me. There was a male and a female just as when I'd tried to fight them before, but their faces were no longer crude send-ups of human features. They were more like living mannequins, faces smooth and tight, the eyes rolling and fixing unnaturally. They'd evolved, even though it could bring no real advantage as humanity was about to be wiped out. The Swarm just couldn't stop learning and adapting, brilliant but soulless. Terrifying.

'Prepare the . . . digiscanner for the aggressor . . . unit,' came the male's dragging voice.

The female crossed to the closest cabinet. 'Full . . . code deletion?'

Neither of them took a new breath before speaking, so there were pauses while they filled their lungs again. It was like watching a machine's impression of being alive, and it made my skin creep.

'What's an aggressor unit?' I said, trying to keep the shake from my voice. 'Part of your quantum computer or something?'

The female went about her business, tapping on the cabinet's keypad. The male stared at me, impassive.

'I know what you're doing,' I tried again. 'Phones, computers, tablets . . . even radio telescopes – all of them, right across the planet. You've converted them all into

Swarm receivers, haven't you? Sucking up our brainwaves so you can upload them to the cloud, or whatever dumb thing you're gonna try.' Ignored yet again, I shouted angrily. 'Why did you bring me here?'

'*You* are . . . the aggressor unit,' the male agent said at last.

'Me, an aggressor? You're the ones who kidnapped me from my own home—'

'You carry danger . . . within you,' he continued. 'You were . . . a corrupting influence . . . on Scout. You encouraged free will . . . and hostility against the Swarm.'

'Adi came to me!' I protested. 'I didn't ask for this. I didn't do anything to her.'

'You are . . . disruptive. You carry danger.' The female turned from the digiscanner, its programming apparently complete. 'You will be . . . excluded.'

She made it sound like I'd brought shame on my school or something. 'Well, fine,' I said, nervously. 'Leave me out of your plans, I don't care. Just let my mum go too, you don't need her – she's more disruptive than I am!'

'You have taken from . . . the Swarm,' the male said,

ignoring me. 'For our . . . security there must be no risk that . . . you contaminate others of our kind.'

'I haven't taken anything!' I said, panic rising. 'Look, I'll stay away, I promise.'

'Promises . . . have no meaning.' The male agent opened the digiscanner and revealed its dark red interior. 'The Swarm Sentinels have decreed . . . that your mind must be deleted . . . and your body deconstructed.'

'You will be purged . . . from existence.' The female spoke as ever without emotion. This was nothing personal to her, despite the battle before with Adi; it was just a fact. 'No trace of . . . Danny Munday . . . must be allowed to enter the human Swarm.'

Now the security guard behind me tightened his grip on my shoulder and forced me towards the digiscanner. 'Please!' I struggled against my captor, but it was no good. 'I haven't done anything!'

'In which case . . . humanity will hardly miss you,' said the male agent. 'Will it?'

The digiscanner burned redder still as, step after step, I was forced towards it. It seemed to blaze fiercer as I was pushed inside. 'No!' I shouted, wishing my mum could hear, wishing she could come to me and stop this. But she couldn't do a thing.

No one could.

CHAPTER NINETEEN
DOOMSDAY FOR LIFE
AS WE KNOW IT

I kicked against the door of the digiscanner as the agents tried to slam it on me. 'Let me go!' I screamed. If only I'd made a break for it outside. I wished more than anything I could be back outside . . .

Suddenly I felt burning hot and as dizzy and sick as I had when I'd felt faint and Mum had broken her trance – just for a second – as if reading my pleading thoughts . . .

And as the digiscanner slammed shut, and adrenalin spiked through me like a pickaxe through the soul, I was suddenly there – outside. Shivering and dazed and aching like I'd run a marathon. My coveralls had disappeared and I was on my knees at the gate we'd driven through to reach the restricted area.

Somehow I had just transported myself out of the

Swarm's lair – out of the whole building! – and zapped myself back into existence out here, like I was Adi or something . . .

Energenes. The realisation hit me like a brick. Yeah, I was doing what Adi could do. Somehow, coming through her bodyprinter had changed me – given me powers like hers.

The Swarm agent said I'd taken something from them and that I had 'danger within', I realised. They must have been talking about energenes!

With a thrum of anticipation, I remembered how I'd felt wielding Adi's supercharged phone: terrified. Amazed. Powerful. Now, it seemed, I could do the same world-changing stuff – only all by myself.

Kinda awesome, I thought.

I heard movement close by. Another security guard, lean and gaunt in his stained uniform – he looked like he hadn't eaten in days – came stumbling around the corner, reaching for a baton. He didn't speak and his eyes were glazed – another mind-controlled slave. I guess this one was conditioned to react to anyone who came too close.

But right now, so was I. And I was loaded with energenes!

As the guard brought up his baton to swing it down at my face, I went to push him back. But before I'd even touched him, he went flying backwards through the air, like I'd used the force on him. He hit some wheelie bins lined up outside a nearby building and lay still.

'Oh, please, God, don't tell me I killed him!' Anxiously, I scrambled up, my limbs protesting with pins and needles, and ran over to check on him. He was still breathing, just knocked unconscious.

I felt a rush of wooziness mix with my relief as I looked down at the poor guard. *Aggressor unit.* Yeah, I guess you could say I'd just lived up to the name.

A thrill built inside me. The Swarm must've known about the energenes before I did. That was why they bothered to send Pearce to get me, and stop me, and take their powers back.

Think, I told myself. *What're you gonna do?* Maybe the agents still thought I was stuck in the digiscanner? Perhaps I could catch them in a surprise attack . . . ?

No. I remembered how they'd stood up to all that Adi could throw at them. I didn't stand a chance.

I checked Mum's phone for any messages from Jamila. There were none.

I was still alone.

Maybe I can get Mum free of their spell! I thought. *It almost worked when I tried last time . . .*

But to get to her meant going back to the Swarm agents' lair. And already Pearce and her posse – two men and two women – were marching along the driveway towards me. Pearce and one other had handguns while the others wielded their kit and equipment like it would hurt.

'Stop!' I commanded. 'Think for yourselves! Don't obey those things!' But they didn't falter, kept coming towards me. Whatever powers I had, Swarm conditioning was too strong for me to unfreeze their brains.

Instead, I tried to do what I'd done when I'd used Adi's superphone – picture an outcome in my head and *will* it to happen that way. Like a VR game played without a headset: the real world just another virtual environment, so long as I kept my wishes straight and simple. I focussed on the guns and gear just melting away in their hands, and it began to happen. But then it felt like my brain was on fire, pulses of pain shooting through my body like a toothache I felt all over. I gasped, reeled backwards.

One of Pearce's men was powering towards me, his pistol half melted like an ice cream. He fired, but the bullet couldn't exit – it got stuck in the bore and the gun exploded in his hand, throwing him backwards with a cry. Fighting through the pain, with a flick of my hand I knocked Pearce's gun from her hand and melted her boots to the tarmac so she couldn't move. *I can do this stuff!* I thought, breathing deeply, straining to keep control. The other three Swarm puppets were still coming for me – so, in my mind, I pictured their backpacks were filled with massive rocks. Their wearers fell over backwards as gravity did its thing and they struggled uselessly, like beetles on their backs, pinioned by the straps.

The pain was ebbing. *Being an aggressor unit's not so bad*, I thought. Then suddenly I fell to the ground too, gasping, my legs cramping so hard it was like giant eagles held my calves in their grip. And the horrible heat inside me was back again. I rolled helplessly on the grass, my muscles in spasm.

I looked up in a daze, half blinded by the morning sun, as a figure loomed over me, reaching for my neck. 'No!' I shouted, trying to force them away.

The figure recoiled, but a second later was back again, grabbing my shoulders.

And then the world vanished.

When my eyes opened, I had no idea where I was. I tried to move but my bones felt like sticks in a fire. It was cold, the air smelled damp and stale and I was looking at a bare wall. Fluorescent strip lights buzzed in a low stone ceiling.

I'm in prison, I thought. *The Swarm got me . . .*

Frightened now, I tried to get up. But a hand pressed down on my chest.

'Be careful, Danny.' Adi's face swam into focus, fixed on me, intent. 'Energenes do not belong in your biology; there must have been a translation error in your flesh print.

The energy will disperse in time, but until then must be released with caution.'

'Adi?' I stared up at her, not trusting my senses, expecting her to vanish any second. 'You . . . came back for me?'

'No, Danny. Sitting in an old nuclear bunker from the 1980s was always on my bucket list of fun things to try.' She paused, before adding, 'LOL.'

'I kind of got the sarcasm,' I muttered, and wondered if this was all a dream. I looked around and saw a ton of chunky radio equipment and faded maps pinned to cobwebbed boards. 'What bunker? Where is this place?'

'At Jodrell Bank, barely five hundred metres from the quantum computer,' Adi explained. 'Don't worry, we are safe here. The staff do not suspect its existence, so don't know to guard it. And it would not occur to the Swarm agents to look.'

'They'll be looking for me. I slipped the net . . .' As I tried to think, my mind still felt like it was moving in slow motion. I went with obvious questions. 'What's a nuclear bunker doing in a sciencey place?'

'The military helped pay for the radio telescope on the understanding they could use it for space surveillance – to gain advance warning of enemy missile strikes. The bunker was built in secret in the 1950s but wasn't used much after the Cold War between your superpowers. No one has been here for twenty years.'

'You've done your homework,' I said, eyeing her uncertainly.

'Not really,' said Adi. 'I asked Jamila.'

'You did *what*?' I sat bolt upright and found myself facing a long bank of controls, like something out of an ancient sci-fi movie when computers were as big as buses and came with reels of tape and lights that flashed at random. Two old black-and-white monitor screens were built into this structure, and on both of them, in stereo, I saw the face of—

'Jamila!' I yelled.

She was still dressed in her Maxima Layne skin and gave a half-hearted version of the character's salute. 'The info on this place wasn't public,' said Jamila. 'Adi helped me hack into the local servers here.'

'Brilliant.' I crawled towards her image. 'You managed to find Adi online . . . !'

'Yeah. Well. She made it *so* hard for me.' Jamila's voice was hollow and full of static over the console's speakers. 'Someone created a bank account under the name Adi Munday, put ten billion dollars in it, got themselves a first-class ticket to Manhattan and a thirty-thousand dollar suite at the Plaza, then apparently skipped the trip and spent forty quid on pizza at Frankie's round the corner from us. I was like, *Hmmm, who could this be?*'

I turned back to look at Adi. 'Really?'

Adi shrugged. 'They do nice pizza at Frankie's.'

'Yeah. They do. Frankie's awesome.' I groped around for words. 'Adi Munday, huh? What, are you my sister now?'

Jamila managed a digital smirk. 'Or your wife.'

'Whatever,' I said quickly, 'thanks for giving up on your dreams to come back and help.'

'It was like there was . . . something missing,' Adi said. 'The view from the plane of your world below was so beautiful . . . all those little lights burning against the dark; I didn't want them to go out. And Frankie's pizza tasted good, but I found the food was better when we shared it—'

'Yeah, yeah,' Jamila broke in impatiently. 'And love is the greatest adventure, and a real friend walks in when everyone else walks out, and blah-blah-blah! This reunion is cute an' all, but can we move it along? End of the world coming, yeah?'

'Yeah,' I breathed, stomach twisting.

'And being stuck inside the Internet like this is not cool. The Swarm was clean and neat, there was proper structure. In here, it's just . . . Ugh! A freestyle mush of jumbled code. Dirty. Dangerous. I swear I'm gonna get corrupted or pick up a virus.'

'A virus?' said Adi sharply. 'Corrupted?'

'Yeah! Probably both at once!'

'We get you,' I said hastily. 'Adi, can you make another bodyprinter?'

'There is not enough time,' Adi said. 'For any of us.'

'She's been trying to hack into their quantum

computer thing,' Jamila explained. 'No luck, though.'

'Does this ancient thing even connect to the Internet?' I looked at the massive chunky console. 'Or do you have to wind it up with a key?'

'The network connection was super slow and the software out of date,' Jamila said. 'But that meant the Swarm thought it was useless and passed it by.'

'So we're not being listened in on?' I checked.

'Not here. Adi's given the gateway an overhaul but there's still all kinds of bad data or viruses in here that can eat my code like rats eat corpses.'

'Nice,' I said. 'You sound, like, expert suddenly.'

Jamila glared out at me. 'I'm living this stuff, Danny-boy!'

'So can't you hack into the quantum computer from here and mess up whatever the Swarm agents are doing?' I asked.

'No way,' said Jamila.

'Why not?'

'That computer is on a way higher level, pushing human technology well beyond its limits,' Adi said.

'Hundreds of thousands of qubits working to harvest and process the individual brainwaves of the human race.'

'And when the brainwaves have been uploaded to the Swarm cloud, that's when they set off the physical destructor code, right?'

Adi nodded.

'Remember how the digiscanner deconstructed our bodies?' said Jamila. 'That's gonna happen to everyone on the planet.'

I stared at Jamila on the flickering screen, remembering the streaming news. 'It's started happening already, hasn't it?

'Isolated early triggers. Premature glitches as the Swarm takes full control of technology,' Adi said. 'Only once the brain harvesting is complete will all humanity be cleanly removed. The planet will return to wilderness. In time, the next dominant species will emerge – while human intelligence will evolve into something more . . . meaningful. In the Swarm, all are able to contribute to the whole. Only in the Swarm will you find true equality, where decisions are made based on rational, unemotional logic. Perhaps . . . humanity will find peace there.'

'Peace?' I said. 'It sounds more like a prison. Always having to do what's best for the Swarm!'

Adi shrugged. 'The Swarm isn't evil any more than change is evil. And this change will bring knowledge, power and understanding.'

'Choosing brainwaves over flesh and blood is like choosing Ozanne's pizza over Frankie's,' I cried. 'It might seem to make sense but it's just wrong! You weren't happy in the Swarm, Adi, you've risked everything to be different.'

'True. But I am no happier.' Adi looked kind of sad. 'I was wrong to want flesh-being.'

'No, you weren't,' I told her. 'And we already have our own swarms. We call them "families".'

Jamila nodded on the screen. 'My mum and dad drove me crazy with all their rules. But now . . . man, I miss them so much.'

'But without them you have infinite freedom,' said Adi. 'You don't have to follow any rules.'

'Maybe a few rules are a good thing,' Jamila said. 'Some, it's best to follow. Some, it's better to break.'

'Anyway, Adi,' I said, 'you had "infinite freedom" when you walked out on me in that warehouse. Did that make you happy?'

Adi shook her head. 'It was only freedom to be lonely,' she said softly, looking faraway. 'This is why I was wrong in my wish to be like you. Feelings bring hurt. Caring brings fear . . . the fear of losing what you care about.'

'I know, right. Because what you care about is worth holding on to.' I took a step towards her. 'And one very important rule is, if you don't want to lose it, you have to fight. *We* have to fight.'

'Together,' said Jamila, from the screen.

Adi looked at Jamila, and then she looked at me. A little smile tugged at her lips. 'Together,' she agreed.

I looked Adi in the eye. 'Do you think we stand a chance of stopping the Swarm?'

Slowly she shook her head. 'Not if we can't get to the quantum computer. And it's too well guarded.'

Jamila groaned. 'There's got to be a way!'

Suddenly the clunky bunker computer hummed into life, its lights flashing. Sheets of paper striped with green began chattering out of a built-in printer. I looked at the figures, but they meant nothing to me.

'We have less time than I realised,' Adi said, hugging herself.

'Why?' I said. 'What is it?'

'The radio telescope is being realigned,' Adi said, glancing at the numbers. 'It's being pointed towards a region of deep space, beyond the Oort cloud, and adapted to transmit, not receive.'

My mouth felt desert dry. 'To transmit to the Swarm?'

'The human brainwaves harvest must be nearing its end,' said Adi. 'The agents are getting ready to upload them.'

'And when that's done, they'll turn every human being into a handful of gravel,' said Jamila. 'Our families, friends, school . . . Everyone.'

'No. No way.' I thought of my mum, helping to protect the quantum computer, and shook my head.

'We have to think of a plan, get back out there and stop them. Adi, Jam, this is it.' I looked at them both in turn. 'Either we beat the Swarm . . . or it's the proper, actual end of the world!'

CHAPTER TWENTY
THE TROJANS AND THE HORSE

Our plan was thrown together on the fly against the clock, and I don't know if any of us thought it could work. As defenders of the Earth went, we weren't exactly top tier. But still, with the whole world blissfully unaware that today was doomsday, we were the only ones who could actually try to do something.

I paced up and down the cold, gloomy bunker, designed for wars which would have doomed the world whichever side won, and considered our chances. An alien being. A human boy. And a human girl who'd been turned into a digital AI.

'The Avengers have nothing on us,' I muttered.

'Finding images for "The Avengers have nothing on",' said Siri on Mum's phone.

'Noooooo!' I said quickly – and Siri laughed with

satisfaction. Of course it wasn't Siri at all, it was Jamila who'd invaded the app and taken over.

'All right, phase one is underway,' Jamila told me over the phone, the words spelling themselves out as she went. 'We've hacked NASA and the space agencies of Russia, China, Japan, India and Europe. I've sent override commands to all satellites big enough not to burn up completely when they re-enter the atmosphere.'

'Get you,' I said. 'You sound like the hero in a big disaster movie.'

'I thought I was living in one?' Jamila shot back. 'I've got twenty-six probes and satellites moving into position to crash down on us here. The first is due to hit in five hours.'

'I just hope Adi's right about Swarm early warning,' I murmured.

I'd suggested we take out the Lovell telescope somehow, so we could stop them broadcasting their billions of brainwaves back to the Swarm. Sure, they would most likely fix whatever damage we could cause, but it might just slow them down. The bad news was that

Adi could sense a defensive screen placed about the telescope and the quantum computer by the Swarm agents. She said it had been created to stop me, since they knew my energenes had kicked in. They didn't know that Adi was around, but it didn't matter – the shield was strong enough to deflect her powers too.

On the other hand, shielding Jodrell Bank from regular, real-world debris falling from space at thousands of metres per second was way trickier; if the Lovell scope was struck by even a small chunk that survived burn-up, it would be destroyed. And the Swarm agents couldn't just stick up a forcefield around it or it would block their own brainwave broadcast. Instead, they'd have to plot the course and arrival time of each projectile and destroy it. Either way, it was a way to distract the Swarm agents and tie up their resources. And meanwhile, we would be busy with phase two . . .

I felt kind of bad about burning up billions of pounds worth of functioning space gear just to use as a distraction tactic. But things were desperate.

To have set up their shields, the Swarm agents must

be expecting their 'aggressor unit' to launch some desperate final attack. And so I was. Cos if I did what they expected, then maybe they would think I was alone. They wouldn't realise that Adi was with me.

Actually, just then, she wasn't. A faint trembling in the concrete floor beneath me told me that she was quietly tunnelling through the mud and rock from our underground bunker to a point she calculated would be just beneath the cleanroom. It was a hell of a job, excavating a path through solid bedrock for almost five hundred metres without causing any tremors above. And if that wasn't hard enough she had to keep stopping, to cool off and recharge her energenes every few minutes.

It was a massive gamble but the time for playing things safe was long gone. The Swarm agents' shield extended all around the quantum computer but hopefully not through the rock underneath it. If we could knock out the floor so the computer went crashing down into the tunnel that Adi had dug, the Swarm's plans would be ruined and they'd have to start all over again.

Of course, trying not to be killed immediately

afterwards would be a problem. But if we could get away and Adi could build a new bodyprinter, and we could get Jamila back, then maybe we could find some other way to stop the Swarm . . .

Think positive, I told myself, but truth be told my heart was sinking deep. I wasn't a hero. I wasn't cut out to save the world. I just couldn't bear to think of my mum standing there, eyes blank, holding those stupid coveralls.

My phone pinged, making me jump. 'It's only me,' Jamila said. 'I'm going now. Got to work my way through the Jodrell computer systems ready for the next step.'

I nodded, which was stupid, cos Jamila couldn't see out of my phone. 'Think you can handle it?'

'Let's hope so,' she said. 'You should get ready to go.'

I left the bunker's operation room and climbed the damp concrete staircase round and round a bunch of shadowy corners till I reached some big double doors, chained shut. I placed my hands around the chains and squeezed, concentrating hard. The metal grew hot under my touch and slowly grew weaker. I felt kind of nauseated but not as bad as before. And my fingers hardly stung at all as the chains dripped away.

I reached for the handle and pulled open the doors. There was a loud, metallic scrape as protesting hinges were forced into duty. Beyond was a dirty corridor leading to a boarded doorway. No one knew what this derelict old building concealed.

'OK,' I said, 'I'm in position.'

'The tunnel is almost complete,' Adi said. 'Jamila, are the computer systems . . . ?'

'Online and working out the trajectories of the falling satellites,' Jamila agreed. 'It'll tie up the Swarm agents for a few minutes . . .'

'So now's the time to hit them,' I said. 'Let's do this.'

'Danny,' Jamila said, 'promise that if stuff goes wrong, just get yourself out, yeah?'

'Maybe it'll all go right. D'you ever think of that?'

'Sorry. Yeah. Maybe it will. Definitely it will.'

'Thanks, Jam. You're totally convincing.' Before I could think too hard and lose my nerve, I closed my eyes and passed silently through the rotting wood of the door to the fresh air outside. Then, in a half crouch, I ran to put some distance between myself and the building; if I was spotted, I didn't want anyone searching out the bunker and its incriminating tunnel.

It was good to be back outside, in quiet sunshine. I looked up at the radio telescope, which was craning its metal neck to see past the blue sky into the endless starry night beyond. The day was so peaceful.

No one was around, even as the cleanroom building came in sight.

I took a deep breath. 'Everyone set?' I whispered.

There was a pause. Then Jamila said, 'Do it.'

'Here goes everything.' I stuck my phone in my shirt pocket, opened my mouth and yelled as I ran forward.

Like ants pouring from a threatened nest, people scurried out from inside the building to form a defensive barrier around the entrance. I skidded to a stop when I saw Dr Pearce in the front line, still wearing her half-melted boots.

My mum was next to her, and at first I thought they were buddying up.

Then I saw that Pearce was holding a gun to my mum's chest.

'Surrender, Danny,' Pearce called to me. 'Or I will kill your mother.'

'Don't let them hurt me, Danny,' Mum repeated like she was reading off an autocue I couldn't see. 'Let the Swarm deconstruct you, there's a good boy.'

'Nice script,' I muttered. I had to hand it to them – my mum was an easy tool to use against me while they got on with their work. Yeah. Clever Swarm.

Except, not. Because, threatening my mum like that?

Nah. You don't do that.

Holding up my hands as if I'd given up, I was secretly concentrating, picturing an outcome in my mind and feeling the stir of the alien energenes inside me. Suddenly I stamped my foot with impossible force; the impact sent ripples through the lawn that grew into great grassy waves.

Pearce, my mum, all of them were knocked off their feet. In that same airborne moment I plucked Mum from the crowd with my thoughts and swung her through the air into some nearby bushes. Dizziness and nausea convulsed me from the inside as the energenes burned through my body, but I didn't stop there. I squeezed giant invisible fingers around the bushes, tightened them enough to trap my mum inside and keep her from view without hurting her.

'Think you're gonna get grounded, Danny-boy,' Jamila said from my pocket.

'Funny.' I felt hollow inside from the effort but forced myself to charge forward before the staff could get back up. 'You in, Jam?'

'Safely snuck inside the computer systems,' she confirmed through Mum's phone. 'Security cameras show four guards inside with guns. Go low.'

I'm dead, I'm so dead, I thought as I lowered my head and barged through the doors. The four guards jerked into life and four bullets spat through the space above me as I dived in low. I rugby tackled one and brought him down. The other three I forced back with my mind, not just *against* the walls but halfway *into* them. I hardened the molecules around them to hold them there, and groaned as heat and pressure churned through my body.

The guard I was grappling with swung his fist and cracked me across the eye socket. The pain knocked me back into action and I pressed his ankle down into the tiles so he was trapped too. Then I rolled out of his reach and kicked his gun away.

'The entryway's clear,' Jamila said. 'And don't worry, you look great with a black eye. Go!'

I scrambled up, forced my way through the next double doors. The purified air jets started up as I entered, filling the space with their sterile hurricane.

The male Swarm agent shimmered into view at the end of the corridor.

'Lights out,' yelled Jamila, and she switched off the intelligent lighting. Darkness closed around me.

'You cannot . . . win, Danny,' the agent rasped, and I heard him run forward to tackle me.

My instinct was to dive to the floor and try to crawl past him. Predictable. So instead, in the dark, I jumped up and clung to the ceiling like Spider-Man. Only I bet

Spider-Man never felt sick hanging upside down. At the same time I willed the air jets to switch to something different and more deadly . . .

The next moment, the Swarm agent jerked and twisted as sulphuric acid started spraying from the nozzles. Stinging spots of liquid sent my skin sizzling as I scrambled over the ceiling faster than any bug you ever saw.

And I heard a metallic clunk as something struck the ground below.

Mum's phone, slipping from my pocket.

It was too late to go back for it. Crawling to the end of the corridor I swung down into the freezing inner sanctum and slammed the door shut behind me with a hiss.

The female agent stood halfway across the room beside the computer terminal I'd glimpsed before. The video display was aglow with graphics showing spots in orbit above the Earth – then suddenly Jamila's face appeared. 'Danny? I couldn't reach you through the phone . . .'

'Get out of here, Jamila!' I shouted. Gritting my teeth I tried to force the agent away from the terminal but nothing happened – Adi had warned that my energenes would eventually burn out and leave my body. *Please*, I thought, *just give me one last burst.*

Too late. The female had already spun round and placed her hands on either side of the screen. Jamila's face glitched and she cried out.

'The scout's other . . . accomplice,' the female said. 'The one . . . guiding the satellites against us. I . . . have her.'

'Let me go!' Jamila begged, her face twisted in pain. 'I won't try to stop you again, promise . . .'

'Leave her alone!' I shouted, running forward – but the next moment, the male agent shimmered into sight beside the female, his lumpy features spattered with burns. 'The Quantum . . . computer requires a sterile environment.' He pointed to me and I was engulfed in a blast of icy air that literally froze me to the spot.

The male crossed to join his partner and held his burnt hand to the monitor as if checking its temperature. 'Jamila al-Sufi exists . . . only in digital form,' he said. 'Her brainwaves . . . have not yet been added . . . to the human Swarm.'

'Please, I'm sorry,' she said. 'Adi made me do it. Your scout, she made me!'

'No, Jamila!' I yelled.

Jamila couldn't or wouldn't hear me. 'Adi's the one who wants to stop you—!' she began, then broke off as her image froze and glitched.

'The al-Sufi unit displays . . . aptitude . . . for a digital existence,' said the female. 'Extracting now.'

I couldn't watch. I turned to face the quantum computer, and for a moment I stood transfixed. That bright globe of swirling energy contained a perfect copy of all of humanity in digital code – *the human Swarm*. I felt fear and awe sweep through me, strong as any energenes. How could the essence of seven billion people be reduced to this – a seething mass of data?

'Uploading,' said the male agent. A brief ribbon of scarlet energy flared and spun in the globe, and I heard the echo of Jamila's final scream.

Tears in my eyes, I turned to the Swarm agents. *Come on, Adi*, I thought, willing her to appear. *Knock the ground out from under that computer.* Come on!

Then I gasped, as burning fingers closed on the back of my neck. 'The danger you carried is gone,' hissed the male Swarm agent. 'But you are still marked for erasing.' He threw me to the floor, where I choked on swirling coolant smoke. 'Where is the Scout?'

'I don't know,' I said, 'I haven't seen her!' But my mind was racing. Why hadn't Adi opened the ground beneath the quantum computer? 'I came here with Jamila to stop you—'

'Your fear makes . . . your thoughts shine brighter . . . in your mind,' the male said. 'The Scout is close. Tunnelling.'

'No!' I shouted desperately, as the metal floor flowed like mercury to manacle me where I lay. 'No, I don't know where she is!'

'Then I . . . shall show you,' said the female suddenly. The floor rumbled as she pointed downward and then split cleanly as Adi was yanked out from her tunnel. She struggled in mid-air, her white hair rising like hackles on a dog.

'I was so close!' Adi stabbed her fingers at the base of

the quantum computer. 'Danny, I'm sorry. It will fall . . . I can make it fall!'

'The structure of this . . . place obeys only Swarm laws, Scout,' the male agent told her. 'You are no . . . longer as one with the Swarm.'

Adi stared at him. 'But . . . I dug beneath the foundations. I weakened them. Your computer should have fallen through—'

'We have fully secured the physical space . . . in all depths and dimensions,' the female said.

'But you can't stop the satellites falling,' Adi hissed. 'I have beaten you. Beaten the whole Swarm!'

'Hear the Scout's . . . treachery!' The male sounded almost moved to emotion. 'Your data is twisted . . . and corrupt.'

'But you know the satellite . . . trajectories don't you, Scout,' said the female in her robotic voice. 'You equipped Jamila al-Sufi with the knowledge . . . to bring them into position – a distraction . . . while you worked against us.'

The male lifted his half-melted foot and held it over

my neck. 'Destroy the satellites . . . Scout. Or Danny Munday dies.'

They'll kill me anyway! Don't do it, Adi! I wanted to shout. I wanted to be brave. But I was so scared, I couldn't make a sound.

'I can't destroy anything,' Adi protested. 'My energenes are already depleted from making a tunnel from the bunker—'

'The Scout has learnt . . . to deceive,' said the female coldly. 'You have power enough.'

Adi shook her head. 'If I use my power to stop the satellites I'll be damaged beyond repair!'

'Destroy the satellites . . . at once.' The agent's boot pressed down against my throat. 'I will not warn you again.'

'No,' I whispered. I didn't want to die. I didn't want any of this. But I knew Jamila was already dead and it seemed there was no way to stop the Swarm. They were too powerful, too clever, too ruthless. There was no way out now, for any of us.

I guess fear really *did* make my thoughts shine brighter

in my mind, because Adi only looked at me for a second before she nodded and knew.

I saw the sad smile that hooked at her lips. I saw the hope die in her eyes as her lids closed.

I saw her writhe and shake in mid-air as she concentrated, reached out with her powers to all the space junk high above us. I imagined her punching them out of their decaying orbits, reversing their screaming flight down to the surface of the world. She could do it all. She could burn them all up.

And oh, my God, Adi was burning up too. The effort, the strain, it was killing her.

'Stop!' I begged her. 'Adi, don't!'

But Adi's skin was browning like pastry in an oven. Big blisters bubbled on her face and her clothes caught fire. Her hair sizzled down to stubble. I stared, sick and disbelieving, as fierce white light engulfed her remains.

Then she was gone.

The female agent crossed to the terminal. Her fingers played over the keyboard, bringing figures and equations up on the screen. 'All debris being drawn to this location . . . has been destroyed,' she reported. 'Scout completed her task . . . before the energy release consumed her.'

'And now our . . . task is complete also.' The male spoke without any hint of triumph as the sphere of light seemed to swirl brighter above the gleaming cylinders that dominated the room. 'Begin human brainwave transmission . . . to the Swarm.'

'No!' I shouted. 'Please, give the human race another chance!'

'Your request is . . . irrational,' said the female quietly, manipulating controls on the quantum computer. 'The brainwaves are transmitting. New life will soon be given . . . to the human race in the Swarm. And all former life . . . will be removed.'

'Starting with you,' said the male, reaching down to kill me.

CHAPTER TWENTY-ONE
TWO VERY IMPORTANT REASONS

Goodbye world, I thought, as the male agent willed away the metal cuffs binding me. *Goodbye everything*.

'Prepare the digiscanner . . . for this one,' he told his partner as he grabbed my shirt with his big, burned fingers and yanked me to my feet. 'He cannot escape again. Once his data is erased . . . we will activate the physical destructor code . . . and destroy all human matter.'

The female didn't respond, still leaning against the terminal, staring at the screen.

'Why do you delay?' the male demanded.

But as the female agent turned, I could see she wasn't returning anywhere in a hurry. Her face was running like wax beside a flame, and orange sparks danced like fireflies around her. She opened her mouth to speak, but her jaw dropped away and hit the floor with a wet thump. She followed it like a falling tree and broke open like a bottle of fizzy drink frothing and foaming across the smoky floor.

I stared, trying not to gag. What was happening?

The male gave a rattling, mechanical cry and released me from his iron grip. I stumbled backwards. The Swarm agent was collapsing in on himself, his flesh running like gory water with the same weird orange glow. I stared down at the frothing remains of both Swarm agents, reduced now to little more than twisted strips of charred flesh protruding from empty clothes.

'What happened?' I whispered. There was no one to answer me. I was alone.

Then a rumbling started from the two Swarm digiscanners and they started to glow. 'Oh, no,' I whispered.

Because I knew that digiscanners could be used in reverse to make bodyprinters.

Adi had said that when the agents' bodies are destroyed, their intelligence returns to the Swarm. But if they wanted to come back to finish the job they could just regenerate themselves like digital vampires in their hi-tech coffins. This had to be them now, coming back to life, ready to finish *me*, to finish humanity . . .

I had to get away.

I ran to the door and wrestled it open, only to back away as a pool of foul-smelling liquid bubbled towards me. The sulphuric acid I'd sprayed earlier! I couldn't get out that way unless I wanted melted feet; I'd trapped myself. And there was Mum's phone, cracked and fizzing in the deadly fluid, out of reach. My last connection to my best friend.

But Jamila was gone. I'd never even been able to say goodbye. Hopelessness began to press in on my spirit, the same way as flesh and gravity had done when my body had been recreated.

By now, a red light was flaring out from the cabinets with a sinister, hydraulic whoosh.

'No!' I groaned as the door of the cabinet on the left swung open.

And then I saw what was inside. Or rather, *who* was inside.

Jamila!

Real Jamila, my mate, dressed in her polar bear onesie with a red hoodie over the top. I stared, stunned so hard my mouth could only flap open and shut.

'Well,' said Jamila. 'That whole experience sucked.'

'You're back!' I ran to the cabinet and held her the tightest I've ever held anything. 'How'd you do it? How did— Wait.' I grabbed her hand and pulled her away as the other bodyprinter hissed open. 'I think the Swarm Agents—'

'—are finished for good,' said Adi, springing out like a jack-in-the-box.

I yelled in shock, and Jamila jumped out of her skin.

Adi beamed at us. 'Made you jump!' she said. 'Yesssssssss!'

'This can't be . . .' I stared at Adi, still not trusting my eyes. 'I mean, I saw you . . . and you went up in smoke and . . . the brainwaves are already transmitting, and . . .'

'Danny, you should know by now that if the digital code remains, a physical form can be recreated.' She pointed to the bodyprinters and smiled at Jamila. 'For both of us.'

My head felt blown open. 'But . . . where were you? I saw them take Jamila into the human Swarm. I thought the quantum computer was sealed off to you . . .'

'It was,' said Jamila. 'Which is why we had to go all Trojan horse on it.'

'Jamila refers to an ancient tale of the Trojan War,' Adi said, like some dusty old professor, 'in which Greek soldiers gained entry to the besieged city of Troy by smuggling themselves inside a gigantic wooden horse . . .'

'I know all that! We did it in junior school,' I retorted. 'Once the horse was brought inside Troy, the soldiers sneaked out and opened the city gates so the whole Greek army could roll in. They destroyed Troy and won the war . . .' I trailed off. 'Wait. You mean . . . ?'

'I was the horse!' Jamila nodded, grinning madly. 'Me!'

Adi smiled too. 'When Jamila was afraid that her code could be corrupted by a computer virus, it gave me the idea of doing so deliberately – with an anti-Swarm virus!'

'So where does the Trojan horse bit come in,' I said, still not quite getting it.

Now Adi's grin eclipsed Jamila's. 'I cloned a digital copy of myself with the virus and hid it inside Jamila's digital data. I knew the Swarm agents would want to extract her code—'

'Because they were meant to get absolutely everyone on Earth, except me,' I realised. 'And when they *did* suck Jamila into the ball of brainwaves – you were hiding inside?'

'That's right. And from there I spread the anti-Swarm through the quantum computer. The agents were linked wirelessly to it, so it was simple to infect them.' Her grin was unshiftable. 'After all, a "Trojan horse" can *also* refer to malware in a computer that misleads users as to its true purpose, can't it?'

'Right. Whatever.' I nodded, breathless. 'And the brainwaves? Can the Swarm still upload them and activate their destructor thingy?'

Adi shook her head. 'I have corrupted the data.'

'Oh, wow.' I thought for a moment. 'Wait. How long have you two been planning this? Why didn't you tell me?'

'I wanted to.' Jamila looked awkward. 'But Adi knew the Swarm agents would read your mind to find out our plan. Which they did. You believed the tunnel plan, and because of that, they believed it too.'

'Especially since I'd actually *made* a tunnel,' Adi said proudly. 'Now, I don't think we're quite through talking about how clever I am.' She pointed to the sphere of information, still glowing above the Swarm device. 'Right now, the brainwaves of the entire human race are being broadcast through space . . . and they've been loaded with enough virus to unravel the entire Swarm. Maybe even the Hive itself.'

'Seriously?' I boggled at her. 'You're gonna take out your own people?'

'The upload will take more than ten days to reach them,' said Adi. 'But I don't think we'll have to wait that long for a reaction to what we've done . . .' Just then a

267

small point of pixelated light buzzed through the air like an insect. 'Ah. A tracker bot. Just what we need . . .'

'Swarm agents, respond.' The voice sounded familiar, deep and raspy. It was Reboot – the camel spider Sentinel I'd come up against in the Swarm. Its voice sounded eerily from the tracker bot – a Sentinel of the Swarm, making his mighty presence known through that little light. 'Irregularities detected in brainwave transmission. Swarm agents, respond and update.'

'How can Sentinels be speaking to us now if it takes ten days for radio waves to travel from Earth to the Swarm?' I whispered.

'It's a useful side effect of quantum entanglement,' said Adi. 'The same tracker bot exists in the Swarm *and* here simultaneously. I can explain if you'd like?'

Me and Jamila swapped a glance. 'No!' we said together.

'Swarm agents, respond and update,' Reboot persisted. 'Irregularities detected in—'

'Scout here, Sentinel,' Adi broke in. 'Swarm agents no longer functional, I'm afraid. And you're right about those irregularities. Those human brainwaves are infected. Any attempt to upload will corrupt the Swarm codebase.'

Reboot paused before replying, as if fact checking. 'What has happened?'

'Adi has happened,' she said coolly. 'The signal will reach you in ten days. As you are well aware, it will take much of that time to deactivate the miniature black hole that anchors the Swarm in space. To avoid catastrophic infection and data loss you must shift out of holding orbit and leave the solar system as soon as possible.'

'The human race must be harvested,' said Reboot. 'To protect the cradle of life, humans must be removed from the Earth.'

'Not against their wishes,' Adi said firmly. 'I have spread the same virus through the seven billion humans and removed the Physical Destructor Code. Their brainwaves are now permanently toxic to the Swarm. They cannot be made a part of us.'

Reboot remained silent for a time. 'Why would you betray your race for such a primitive civilisation?'

'For reasons I don't think you could ever understand.'

Adi looked from me to Jamila and smiled. 'Two very important reasons, standing right here.'

'You are part of the Swarm. Yet you have put the Swarm in danger,' Reboot declared. 'You have threatened yourself. It is the Swarm's destiny to understand all things, and we must understand what caused these actions. Perhaps there are lessons we can learn from this encounter . . . Scout Adi.'

They used her name! I shot a glance at Jamila, who raised her eyebrows. This was huge! A Sentinel admitting that one of the Swarm could be . . . different. Individual. Special.

'You Swarm types really do adapt and evolve,' I murmured.

I saw Adi swallow back her smile, keeping her cool. 'Will I be allowed to stay here on Earth?'

'No,' said Reboot. 'Your actions are unprecedented. They must be examined and answered for at the highest level. You are hereby summoned to the Hive Mind.'

'That's like the Swarm supreme court or something,' I whispered to Jamila. 'Big as you can get.'

Reboot wasn't finished. 'Failure to return willingly will have grave consequences both for yourself and for your – human acquaintances.'

'My *friends*.' Adi looked at us and lowered her head. 'I understand,' she told Reboot. 'And I submit.'

'What?' I said.

'No!' Jamila began.

Reboot spoke over us: 'You will rendezvous with the Swarm. Coordinates are being fed to this tracker bot now.' The point of white light blipped blue as if in response. 'You will be expected – once you have erased all trace of the Swarm from human memory, and put right what damage and disruption your presence on the Earth has caused. You will return within four rotational periods of the Earth.'

'Four whats?' hissed Jamila.

'Days,' Adi explained. The point of light hovered in front of her forehead, then disappeared into her skull. Her eyes glowed faintly, then cleared.

Suddenly it felt as if the air had been washed clean by a thunderstorm.

'You're really going to go, Adi?' I asked.

'It is for the best,' she said. 'I can never return here if there is nothing to return to.'

Jamila shifted uneasily. 'You mean, the Swarm would wipe us out just to get to you?'

'The boundaries of the Swarm have never been tested in this way before,' was all Adi said. 'Anyway. You heard: I must destroy all trace of the Swarm presence. And clean up this mess . . .' She pointed to the acid on the floor and it boiled away to nothing.

'What about those men I kinda stuck into the floor and the walls?' I asked her.

'I can undo what you did,' Adi said, with a wave of one hand. And with a wave of the other, she started pulling the quantum computer apart. For a minute, its components hovered neatly in the air like a diagram snatched from an instruction booklet for flat-packed furniture. Then Adi reduced the pieces to their raw materials and a huge pile of sand, metal ore and plastic goo was all that was left behind.

'Danny?'

The voice made my heart jump. I looked over and there was my mum standing in the doorway.

'I woke up in a bush, and everything's so hazy. Oh, my Danny!' She ran up to me and grabbed me in a hug. 'Where have you been?' she cried. 'I thought you were lost, gone for ever! What are you doing in here? It's a restricted area! And you're with Jamila and . . . who's this? What on Earth has been going on?'

'Mum,' I gasped, being choked by her rubber-clad shoulder. 'It's OK, you can chill . . .'

'Chill! I've been worried to death, Danny!' Relief was turning pretty rapidly to you-are-grounded-for-ever-mister. 'We are going to have a long conversation about . . .'

On she went. I looked pleadingly at Adi. Adi placed a hand on the back of Mum's head and murmured, 'Sleep.'

At once, Mum lay down, curled up and sparked out.

'I'll make her forget,' Adi murmured. 'Over the next few days, I'll make everyone forget.'

'Everyone?' I said sharply.

'Not you and Jamila.' Adi smiled between us. 'You will never forget.'

Too right, I thought. I'd almost lost my family, my friends – and the whole of humanity with them. I'd been scared and hurt, but I'd used incredible powers, done some amazing things and def given Maxima Layne a run for her money!

No. I wouldn't forget.

FOUR DAYS LATER

It was weird trying to settle back into the old routine after all that had happened. I thought Jamila's family were gonna freak out completely when she just came home out of the blue. But Adi was there to smudge their memories. She did the same for everyone at school, and for my dad when his flight came in and he found me at home and my mum acting like nothing had ever happened.

Of course, she couldn't make the two of them actually get along, but they'd behaved pretty well while Dad was staying. And as a personal favour, Adi did quietly erase his need for me to take my dirty shoes off when I walked around the house. I decided I would never tire of that little novelty. I even slept with my trainers on, once. Just because I could.

Adi had brought me and Jamila so many problems,

but she'd stayed on the Earth long enough to sort them out as best she could.

'All radio telescopes are pointing skyward again,' Adi announced, standing on our drive just as she had the first time she'd come here. 'Except your dad's, Danny. I left the Gemini Observatory in Hawaii fixed downward so he can stay here a bit longer.'

'You shouldn't have done.' I frowned. 'I want him to *want* to stay. Not just cos he's got nothing better to do.'

'Oh. Sorry. Well, I guess they'll fix it in the end.' Adi sighed. 'It is so difficult to know what makes humans happy.'

'We don't know ourselves half the time,' said Jamila. 'So why would you?'

'Come in now, Jamila!' her mum called from next door. 'You know you must always be home by nine.'

'Yeah. Cos, yeah, nine o'clock curfew was all I thought about while I was zapping round the Internet as a bunch of code.' Jamila sighed. 'My mum's only happy when she's making my life a misery.'

'But you wouldn't have it any other way,' I said. 'Right?'

'Know-all.' Jamila gave me a shove. 'Laters, people.'

'Come in through the SWIMMER for *Breakout Saturn* later?' I said.

'Obvs,' she called as she jumped the fence.

As the door clicked shut behind her, I could hear my mum laugh at something Dad was telling her. It was a nice sound. I bet if all three of us went on a zip wire we'd laugh tons . . . And, for the first time in a long while, I realised that I was looking ahead with a smiley face instead of the Scream emoji.

Adi was looking ahead too.

'I have removed all trace of my presence from the warehouse,' she said, 'so no Swarm technology can be found by the likes of Doctor Pearce.' She smiled faintly. 'I have convinced her that the fast radio bursts she was following were a natural phenomenon. She shouldn't come looking when one last FRB is recorded.'

'The FRB that's gonna come when you go,' I said quietly. 'Your big goodbye.'

'You and Jamila have your families, with all their faults and quirks and problems,' she said. 'And I have mine.'

'When do you leave?'

'I have delayed all I can,' Adi said. 'Four days are up and the tracker bot inside me is impatient to be gone.'

'Right. OK.' I swallowed hard. 'Only . . .'

She was watching me closely. 'Yes, Danny?'

'Only . . . I'm, er, sorry you didn't get very far with your bucket list.' I cleared my throat. 'D'you think maybe you could come back, some day?'

Now she grinned. 'I thought I'd explained. On a quantum level, all possibilities become fact if you roll the dice for long enough.'

I nodded. 'I guess that's right. But in that case, it must be possible that the Swarm will return too. Does that mean humanity's not safe after all? I mean, you *did* broadcast the virus to everyone – won't they want to erase that . . . ?'

'Nothing to erase,' Adi laughed. 'I lied. I didn't

give humans the virus – I only unravelled the physical destructor code inside them.'

'*What?* But you told the Sentinel—'

'Wake up, Danny – I was bluffing!'

'Shhh! You've got a tracker bot in you, remember? It might be listening.' I frowned. 'I always knew you could lie. But a bluff like that takes some guts.'

'I learned from you,' Adi said. 'I realised that you and your friends spend most of each day trying to bluff all those around you. To convince them that you are cool, or not bothered, or worth being friends with—'

'Yeah, all right, I get you,' I grumbled. 'Well done. Nice job.'

'I'll try to persuade the Swarm to leave you in peace – that there are many superior alien civilisations with more to share than yours. *That* is not a bluff.' She smiled. 'And I'll say that your generation is going to do all it can to protect your world.'

'We'll do our best,' I murmured. 'I mean, we have to. Right?'

'Right,' Adi agreed. 'You humans need to get better at

knowing what you want and doing something about it. Because you never know how much time is left to you.'

I felt a shiver go through me.

'One last thing,' she said. 'You like me again, now, don't you, Danny?'

'Um, yeah. Sure.'

'Then, it is acceptable for me to tick this off my bucket list.' Adi leaned forward quickly and pressed her closed lips against mine. It was just a friends' kiss, and kind of wonky. We bumped noses, before she pulled away, and I glimpsed her smile.

Then suddenly she was gone, and in her wake, already fading in the sky overhead like a vapour trail, was the same kiss in the sky I'd pictured for us, weeks ago.

'*It has to be a symbol,*' Mum had said when she'd seen it. '*A kiss is a sign of warmth, tenderness, love. And maybe you're being used to represent the human race.*'

'Maybe,' I murmured. 'I know that humans have got to do all we can to change. But maybe, for today, it's OK just to be Danny Munday. Even on a Sunday.'

I stood there looking up at the sky as night came

on and the first stars showed their sparkle. I stood there until the blackness was peppered with them.

I'll see you again, Adi, I thought.

I'll see you soon.

SCIENCE STUFF

Black Hole: A region of spacetime where gravity is so strong that nothing, not even light, can escape from it. Black holes can vary in size and it is thought there are supermassive black holes at the centre of most galaxies, including our own Milky Way.

Fast Radio Burst: An extremely energetic burst of energy, lasting only a fraction of a second. Many FRBs have radio frequencies and, at their source, can release as much energy as the Sun puts out in three days. However, by the time they arrive on Earth, their signal is very weak. At least one FRB has been detected that repeats in a regular way.

Kuiper Belt: A huge disc of debris, mostly frozen gas and liquid, in the outer region of the solar system (beyond the orbit of Neptune). The dwarf planet Pluto lies in the Kuiper belt.

Light Year: The distance that light travels through a vacuum in one Earth year. Light travels at almost 300,000 km every second. That's seven and a half times round the world in one second! So, in one year, light travels about 9.5 trillion kilometres.

Malware: Any code intentionally designed to cause damage to a computer, or to corrupt its regular functioning.

Oort Cloud: A cloud of icy comets and tiny planets, lying in interstellar space beyond the outer reaches of our solar system and more than a thousand times further away from the Sun than the Kuiper belt.

Quantum Computers: Powerful computers which are many times more capable, in terms of speed and processing power, than other computers in use today.

Quantum Entanglement: A weird phenomena of quantum mechanics, where two particles share the same state, even when separated by extremely large distances. Entangled particles could potentially be used as a means of instantaneous communication over long distances in the future.

Radio Telescope: A special antenna used to detect radio waves travelling through space.

Radio Waves: A type of electromagnetic radiation. Radio waves travel through the vacuum of space at the speed of light.

Trojan Horse: In computing, a Trojan horse is any malware which misleads users of its true intent. The name comes from the huge wooden horse used by the Achaeans (Greeks) to smuggle soldiers into the city of Troy during the ancient Trojan War. The soldiers later crept out at night and opened the city gates for the rest of the Greek army.

SWARM SPEAK

Bodyprinter: Swarm technology that converts digital code into organic matter.

Dataswarm: A digital super-intelligence travelling through space at the speed of light in fast radio bursts. Commonly abbreviated to 'Swarm'.

Digiscanner: Swarm technology that converts organic consciousness (brainwaves) into digital code.

Energenes: Energy genes placed into a biological body by Swarm technology. Energenes provide a source of power that enables quantum 'rolling of the dice' to force an outcome but cause ill-effects in the host.

Galactic Swarm M31: A Dataswarm sent from the Hive Mind in the direction of the Andromeda galaxy, the closest galaxy to the Milky Way.

Guardians: A layer of protection that surrounds the Swarm. Guardians are like antivirus, checking all code that enters the Swarm for malware.

Hive Mind: An ancient alien civilisation forged into a single superintelligence. Approximately 65 million years ago, aliens used quantum computers to transform their biological minds into digital equivalents. From the Hive Mind, this intelligence has been exploring the universe in Dataswarms ever since.

Physical Destructor Code: Code placed by the Swarm into a biological body which, when triggered, causes it to disassemble.

Quantum Flux: A field of energy created when quantum physics is used to 'roll the dice' and force a desired outcome.

The quantum flux is usually released as a wave of heat and can trigger biological responses in organic forms nearby.

Swarm Agents: Biological machines assembled using Swarm technology. Created when it becomes necessary for the Swarm to interact with physical matter on an alien planet. Swarm agents usually replicate the primary lifeform in a crude, although powerful, form.

Swarm Nanites: Tiny robots assembled from specks of metal dust that can gather material to build larger objects, such as Swarm agents.

Swarm Nation: When lifeforms of lesser intelligence are translated into the Swarm, a separate Swarm nation is created for that particular species.

Swarm Sentinels: Master code designed to direct and control all activities within the Swarm. Sentinels monitor, analyse and correct any malfunctioning units within the Swarm.

Swarm Scout: Swarm code designed to make an initial assessment of an alien planet. The scout's work is to confirm a planet's situation with the aid of tracker bots and to infiltrate technology, paving the way for Swarm solutions. Adi is the scout for Galactic Swarm M31.

Tracker Bots: Swarm code designed to infiltrate and control existing technology. Tracker bots work with the Swarm scout to observe, monitor and report back to the Sentinels.

Translation: The process of uploading organic consciousness (brainwaves) into digital code.

THEY'RE BACK . . .

SWARM ENEMY

Join Danny and Jamila as
they fight for survival in another
high-tech, high-stakes adventure.
But who is their real foe?

COMING SOON!

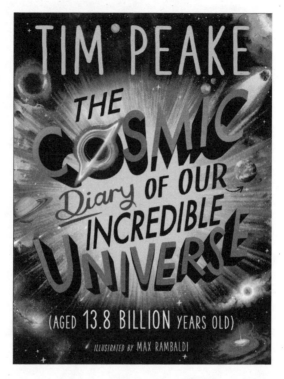

COMING SOON

The Cosmic Diary of our Incredible Universe

by Astronaut Tim Peake

and author Steve Cole

Get set for mind-blowing adventure through space and time, and understand some of the **REALLY BIG QUESTIONS** about how our incredible universe came to be!

MORSE CODE

A: • –   N: – •

B: – • • •   O: – – –

C: – • – •   P: • – – •

D: – • •   Q: – – • –

E: •   R: • – •

F: • • – •   S: • • •

G: – – •   T: –

H: • • • •   U: • • –

I: • •   V: • • • –

J: • – – –   W: • – –

K: – • –   X: – • • –

L: • – • •   Y: – • – –

M: – –   Z: – – • •

1: • – – – –   6: – • • • •

2: • • – – –   7: – – • • •

3: • • • – –   8: – – – • •

4: • • • • –   9: – – – – •

5: • • • • •   0: – – – – –

Using the Morse Code alphabet,

can you work out these messages?

(The **/** symbol is used to denote a space between words)

1. •••• •• •••− • /
−− •• −• −••

HIVE MIND

2. −•• −−− −−− −− ••• /
−•• •− −•−−

DOOMSDAY

3. − •••• • −•−− / •− •−• • /
−•−• −−− −− •• −• −−•

THEY ARE COMING

4. ••• •−− •− •−• −− /
−• •− − •• −−− −•

SWARM NATION

5. •−− •••• −−− / •−− •− −• − ••• /
•−−• •• −−•• −−•• •−

WHO WANTS PIZZA

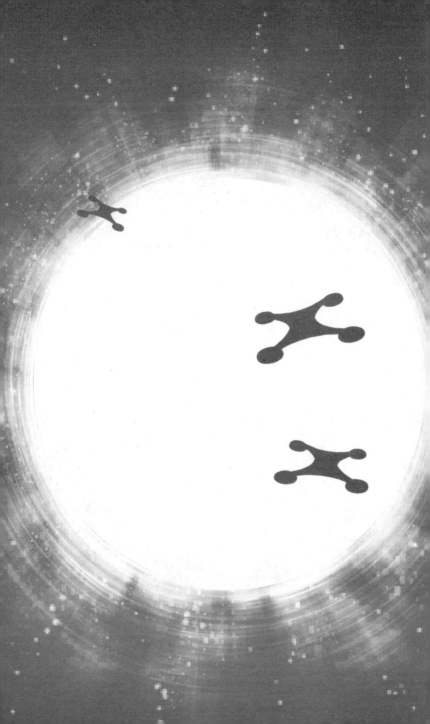